SHADOW LORDS
&
GET OF FENRIS

BY ERIC GRIFFIN &
GHERBOD FLEMING

WORLD OF
DARKNESS
www.worldofdarkness.com

Oksana had performed the favor that Child Marrow had asked. She could hardly refuse and kindle the disfavor of the Sun-Curser, but loyalty among the tribe was hardly monolithic. There were many stormcrows and many masters, all of whom sought to please Grandfather Thunder in their own fashion.

"Are you hungry, Oksana Yahnivna?" a voice asked her from not far away. Oksana's focus shifted from the entrancing flames to Gennady, who stood beside her. He held a strip of venison, still sizzling from the fire. "Have you eaten?" he asked her.

In the past, Oksana had seen Gennady as a towering reddish-brown man-wolf; she had seen him hunt and kill and revel in the blood of his prey. At those times he was fully Garou, approaching the magnitude of spirit that Dawntreader demonstrated daily. Yet at times like this, facing his man-from, his *boy*-form, she saw a tentative, unsure cub, anxious to please. How could Sergiy suffer this whelp? she wondered. Why did Dawntreader encourage such *weakness*?

She snatched the strip of venison from the boy's hand and tore the meat between her teeth, ignoring the searing grease that burned her fingers and mouth. "Leave me be," she said. And Gennady, without protest, without challenge, backed away.

Where was Dawntreader? she wondered. If he were truly strong, he would not sap the spirit of his people with foolish talk of service and humility. If he were truly strong, she thought, he would not trust an advisor of the Shadow Lords who was bound to betray him.

Oksana spat the bite of meat into the fire and threw the rest of the strip onto the ground. She stalked into the darkness, away from the fire. When the sounds of revelry were but a distant echo, she stopped and removed the leather cord that bound her hair.

SHADOW LORDS

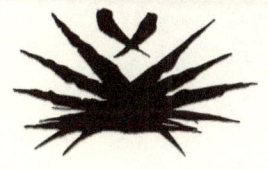

CONTENTS

Chapter 1

By the time Yaroslav Neyizhsalo reached the edge of the village, he stood upright and walked on two high-booted feet, human feet, as any of the villagers might have. Not that a villager would see him—not on the path nor slipping through the deserted streets. Sister Luna was all but hidden tonight; Yaroslav would accomplish the deed set before him soon, when her countenance was absent completely from the sky.

Despite the urgency of his task, Yaroslav did not rush. The royal blood that flowed through his veins was also patient blood; his line had suffered countless betrayals over the ages, and each small revenge was a draught of sweet wine to savor. There would be time enough after the final battle to revel with abandon and wallow in the dregs. For now, the plans were laid, and all that remained was to set them in motion.

The shadows were deep throughout the village, tucked as it was amidst the Carpathian ridges. Sparse light filtered around drawn curtains in the insular cottages but could not keep the night, and all that it concealed, at bay beyond each family's threshold. Yaroslav made his way silently among stands of spruce and fir, keeping a cautious distance from pens of live-stock to avoid fretting the domesticated beasts. Chimney smoke from a few of the houses tainted the air, and on the smoke rode a scent other than that of seasoned firewood, a scent barely noticeable were one not expecting it. Yaroslav followed the odor to its source: a particular house, fairly indistinguishable from those nearby; a plastered affair with diamond patterns etched in the walls; rippled tin roof; painted woodwork that during the day would show bright and colorful, but at night was washed pale violet by the starlight. A low picket fence enclosed tidy flower and vegetable gardens. Behind the house stood several modest wooden outbuildings.

Yaroslav shunned the front walk and slipped around to the back door. It was unlocked. He let himself in and made his way through the cramped kitchen, past the wood-burning cookstove, and to the larger, dimly lit front room where an old man sat carving in a straight-backed wooden chair. There was a ceramic oven in the room, as well. The smoky scent Yaroslav had followed was very pronounced here; the sharp, earthy tang of smoldering wormwood filled the room to the point that breathing was difficult.

The old man looked up from his carving. In the light of the kerosene lantern at his side, his face was gaunt and hollow, craggy as a windswept peak. He saw Yaroslav—the visitor's dark cloak almost hid him from view even at these close quarters, but the old man saw—saw, and returned without comment to his carving. His fingers were long, with bulging joints, but deftly handled the knife that whittled a piece of beechwood into the shape of an animal, a goat. Beneath the old man's chair, an entire herd of beechwood goats languished in a heap, someday perhaps to be traded in one of the larger towns, or even sent as far as Uzhhorod. A blanket was spread before him on the floor to catch his shavings.

"You'd do best not to look away, grandfather," Yaroslav said, irritated at being ignored.

"I am not your grandfather," the old man said without looking up. With a flick of his knife, a wood shaving sailed beyond the blanket and struck Yaroslav's boot.

Yaroslav felt a stirring within him; he repressed the growl that formed deep in his throat. Crushing the shaving beneath the sole of his boot, he stepped farther into the room, towering over the old man.

The old man looked up through rheumy eyes and shrugged at the implied threat. "I have lived many years. The world would not miss me, nor I it. You, however," he poked Yaroslav with the horns of the partly-formed goat, "would miss me. All your work would be for naught without me, wouldn't it?"

"You presume much, grandfather. I attempt to show you

proper respect. You'd do well to return that sentiment."

"Respect!" the old man scoffed. "You see a worn, withered shell, and so you call me grandfather. This is respect? Are you so worthy of respect, wolfling? Does Mother Gaia look kindly upon those who conspire to murder their brethren?"

Yaroslav did growl this time. "You know nothing of who my true brethren are, you cur! Nor of the kind of respect you court," Yaroslav said menacingly. "The years have addled your mind."

The old man stifled a chuckle and returned to his carving, unmindful of the wrath seething before him. "What is your name, wolfling?"

Yaroslav lunged forward. With one hand he grabbed the wrist of the old man's knife hand, and with the other pressed his own, larger blade to the old man's throat. "You will speak to me in a manner befitting my station," Yaroslav said through clenched teeth. "Do you understand? If you do not, no matter how much my plans hinge upon you, our working relationship will be incredibly brief."

The old man's eyes narrowed. He returned Yaroslav's glare for a long moment, then: "What is your name?" His voice was neutral now, with but a hint of distaste; gone was all trace of sarcasm.

Yaroslav held his position several seconds longer, then stepped back and sheathed his blade. "I am Yaroslav Ivanovych Neyizhsalo."

The old man rubbed his throat and scowled. "I will call you Yaroslav Vovkovych. You are all Vovkovych to me, sons of the wolf."

Yaroslav did not care for the appellation, nor his host's recalcitrant manner, but the old man was right about one thing: Without him, Yaroslav's task would become practically impossible. So Yaroslav must refrain from carving out the arrogant old fool's heart, no matter how tempting. It was enough, for the moment, that the old man was not openly disrespectful.

"So," the old man said, "I have grown wormwood in my garden and burned it for many weeks so that you could find me when you were ready. Now you are ready? At last?"

Yaroslav ignored the jibe. He would not be baited; he would settle with the old man later. After. "The time is at hand," Yaroslav said. "Summon the others, and I will return at this time tomorrow night."

The old man nodded. "It will be done, Yaroslav Vovkovych. I will need that much time. The mine I call them from is a full day to the west." Then, slowly, a twisted smile crept over his haggard features, revealing his yellowed teeth to good effect. "'In times of anxiety, one turns to Gaia,'" he intoned the ages-old proverb. "But you, Vovkovych, you turn to me."

"It is you who should be anxious, grandfather," Yaroslav said. He left with the smell of burning wormwood clinging to his hair and clothing, and the sound of the old man's quiet laughter ringing in his ears.

Chapter 2

The knock sounded at the door before dawn had fully broken. "He is here, Oksana Yahnivna," the attendant called from outside the cabin.

Oksana savored her first waking breath. The morning was crisp, as had been the night. Despite the shutters over the windows, and being unexpectedly roused from sleep, Oksana was aware of the precise time of day: Sister Luna, barely peeking down at the world, had retired several hours ago, and Oksana herself much more recently. She took another deep breath and rubbed her face.

"Oksana Yahnivna?"

"Bring me a basin," she called.

"I have one."

Oksana snarled at the closed door. She should have known that the boy, Gennady, would attempt to ingratiate himself with her so. She pulled back her blankets and stood enveloped by the cold morning. "Enter."

Gennady stepped inside bearing the basin of water from the spring. He averted his eyes, intimidated by Oksana's nakedness. Or perhaps it was merely Oksana, naked or clothed, who intimidated him. The boy seemed disconcerted by the fact that she despised him.

"Leave it," Oksana said, stretching, her hands reaching toward the ceiling. "And tell them that I will be along presently." The boy nodded and scurried on his way. How unseemly, Oksana thought, for a full-blooded Garou to play handmaid—if any of these Children of Gaia could be said to be full-blooded Garou. Oksana had her doubts. Bringing washwater was work for Kinfolk. She had said as much to Sergiy, but he was of the opinion that menial tasks were productive for the newly changed, teaching the value of service and humility. Degradation, Oksana thought, was useful only for those who planned on being degraded. Combat produced skilled warriors; capable tutelage empowered worthy advisors.

With a roughspun cloth and the water Gennady had brought, Oksana bathed. She washed the sleep from her eyes and the dust from her body. Goosebumps rose on her skin; an electric rush invigorated her. Sergiy called the spring water the tears of Gaia, welling up from the earth. He had found the aquifer. The Galliards sung that he'd wept and, in sharing the pain of Mother Gaia, had called forth her tears. All this after the death of the Hag. Regardless of Sergiy's eccentricities and his strange ideas about humility, Oksana could not argue with the fact that the land required healing, and the spring ran strong and pure.

Teach *that* to your cubs, Oksana had urged him: how to purify the Mother and strengthen her against their enemies. Not how to bring washwater and change bedclothes.

Cleansed and fully awake now, Oksana put on a silk tunic, sturdy woolen jerkin and pants over that, and boots. Her straight, dark hair, still damp, she pulled back and tied with a leather cord attached to an unusually dark and clouded amethyst. Finally, she wrapped about her shoulders a cape of lynx fur that warmed her and turned away the spring chill.

The meadow, as Oksana made her way to the spring, was calm in the morning light. The Sept of the Dawn, for most of its members, was named metaphorically. The Garou tended to hunt and revel late into the night. Sunrise was an event that many could claim not to have witnessed in many years. Oksana normally counted herself among that number. The grand elder of the sept was one of the few who regularly basked in the first rays of Brother Sol, and Oksana would have been perfectly content to leave that particular routine to him. The glory of sunrise was not what brought her out at this hour.

She found the grand elder at the giant willow by the spring. Sergiy Dawntreader was a massive man with a wild mane of flaxen hair. His legs were as thick as mature elms, and his bare, muscled arms almost as large. Most noticeable, however, were his eyes, light and ethereal as a storm-cleared summer sky. He had a way with his gaze of taking in all of a person, as might the spring a bather. Dawntreader was not alone. He, his guest, and two others rested on low seats of willow, not carved, but formed from the knobby roots of the giant tree as they emerged from the ground then twisted back down into the earth.

The guest was none other than Lord Arkady of the House of the Crescent Moon, preeminent line of European Silver Fangs. Arkady wore elegant silks, leather vest and breeches, and black knee-high boots. A sparkling grand klaive rested at his side. His coloring was dark, but not so much as Oksana's. He seemed slightly affronted that she, Dawntreader's trusted advisor, had not arrived more quickly.

"Lord Arkady," said Sergiy in his deep rumbling voice that caused ripples to form on the surface of the spring, "I present to you the esteemed Oksana Yahnivna Maslov of our brethren the Shadow Lords."

Arkady rose and bowed graciously. "Forgive me if I have disrupted your sleep, Oksana Yahnivna," he said by way of thinly veiled rebuke.

"Had we known more precisely of your arrival," Oksana said, returning Arkady's bow, "I am sure Sergiy Dawntreader would have arranged for the entire sept to be present and proclaim your great deeds."

"Lord Arkady alerted us that he would be coming," said one of the two other Garou present, Victor Svorenko, a Silver Fang fosterling from the Firebird Sept, and the reason for Arkady's embassy. Svorenko always struck Oksana as at least slightly peevish—and often more than slightly. At times, she repented of the fact that it was her advice that had brought him, as well as the fifth Garou, Arne Wyrmbane, to the Sept of the Dawn.

"We know also that the Apocalypse is coming," Oksana said dryly, "but without a more definite announcement, there is much debate regarding the exact time and manner of the arrival."

Svorenko sputtered before again finding his voice. "How dare you jest about such matters!"

Oksana fixed him with a steely glare. She considered

holding her tongue, but showing deference to Lord Arkady was troubling enough; this younger Fang tried her patience beyond measure. "I do not jest, little one. Nor do I fear to speak of that which confronts us each day and night. Perhaps when you are older and have seen more you will better understand such things."

Svorenko began to rise to his feet but was checked by Dawntreader's raised hand. To the young Silver Fang's surprise, the elder began to laugh. His hearty chuckle caused the leaves of the willow to sway, as if sharing his mirth.

"Be calm, my pup," Sergiy Dawntreader laughed. "Young Svorenko guards his kinsman's honor where there is no need. I ask you, does the baker steal the loaf? And now he bristles at me calling him pup. Again I say, be calm. We are among friends here. Feel the warmth of the sun and drink the goodness of the spring, and remember that all glory is to Gaia."

Svorenko, dissuaded but hardly soothed, eased back into his seat. Oksana, too, sat, she at the left hand of Dawntreader, a place of honor, as was Arkady's seat to the right. The younger Silver Fang, she thought, might be one who *would* benefit from a diet of menial labor, if humility were to be learned. But not even Sergiy would convince a Silver Fang of such. Victor would renounce his fosterage and return to Russia rather than accept accommodations beneath his station. As would Oksana, if in his place—though she would remember her own standing and hold her tongue in the presence of elders.

At least the upstart hadn't put a hand to the klaive he wore at his belt; that would have been an insult even good-natured Sergiy could not have overlooked. That Svorenko carried the silver blade at all was testament to the injudicious pampering of the Fangs. The klaive, Victor had informed anyone who would listen shortly after he'd arrived at the caern, was a gift from his cousin, Lord Arkady.

More the fool, him, Oksana had thought at the time—a belief that had only been strengthened since, including this morning.

"Be still," Dawntreader said with his powerful voice, "and know that Gaia is mother to us all." Prompted by the earnest veneration that was palpable in his words, the Garou *were* still, and silent. At that moment, a westerly breeze arose, but it did not feel cold because the sun was just then climbing above the horizon to the east, beyond the lower end of the meadow. Oksana loosened her lynx cape and drank in the warmth. A symphony of sparrows and mourning doves welcomed the dawn, and their song was joined by the rustling of the willow leaves above the Garou's heads.

Wild-haired, towheaded Sergiy rose, eyes closed, and stretched his arms wide. His reach could easily have encompassed his four companions, but Oksana felt that Dawntreader wished to grasp the morning itself, to possess it and hold it to his breast. If anyone could, he would be the one, she thought. He was so strange to her—this hulking Garou who greeted each dawn with such ardor; he was as giant and content as the towering willow. Strange, and so different from her, too, and from her kind, who longed for the comforting embrace of darkness.

"Ahhh," Sergiy sighed aloud.

Oksana felt herself exhale with the grand elder; she heard the others do the same. She could see by their expressions that they, like her, had not previously realized that they'd taken in the new morning, breathed it into their beings, as deeply as Dawntreader—and held that breath.

"Gennady," Sergiy called and, in a moment, the young Garou was there.

He bore a tray of earthenware mugs filled with spring water for the five in attendance beneath the willow. He brought, too, a wide wooden bowl brimming with *vyshnyas,* which was passed around. Oksana took a handful of the cherries and ate them one at a time, each succeeding burst of vibrant, tart juices pursing her lips but leaving her mouth watering for more. She could not help but notice the expression of understated rapture on Sergiy's face as he ate of the fruit. For him the breaking of the fast was more than a satisfaction of the need for sustenance; it was an homage to Gaia, a sampling of her wondrous bounty.

The spring water was the perfect compliment to the sour *vyshnyas*—crisp, cleansing. By the time the group had finished their modest meal, a pleasing languor had taken hold of Oksana. She was warm and content; her resentment of the Fangs, if not ameliorated, seemed a burden for another time. Let little Victor show off his klaive; most likely in his posturing he'd accidentally emasculate himself, and there would be one less lordling to breed.

"I can see by Oksana Yahnivna's smile that she is daydreaming," Sergiy said cheerfully. "Ah, but now I have made her self-conscious. Perhaps it is rest that we all require. Lord Arkady has traveled far. Let us seek peace in dreams. Peace, rest, and renewal. For tonight we will hunt, and tomorrow at dawn we will honor our fosterlings and our guest. Lord Arkady, as befitting an esteemed patriarch of the Silver Fangs and grand elder of the Firebird Sept, will assist in our Rite of Accomplishment for young Victor Svorenko. Until the time of our hunt, then, as always, go with Gaia."

Oksana returned shortly thereafter to her cabin. Despite the sun's rising and burning more fiercely in the eastern sky, the lethargy of the spring and the willow clung to her. Inside again, she undressed and climbed back into bed. There were matters that required her attention. Tonight would be far too busy—Arkady's arrival guaranteed that—but such would simply have to be the case, she decided, as she gave up trying to keep her heavy eyelids from fluttering closed.

Chapter 3

Lightning flashed in the distance, but above the Sept of the Night Sky there were no clouds. Several seconds passed before the rumble of thunder reached Laszlo's ears. The storm was far away. For now.

Perhaps the roiling clouds would skirt the sept and continue eastward toward the Ukraine, or it could be that the wind would usher them north, into Slovakia. More likely, Laszlo knew, the storm would smash itself against the Carpathians and scour the Leech-infested mountains with its fury. There were few calamities beneath the heavens that had spared the sept over the years. Let the wind and the rain and the lightning come, Laszlo thought. The Garou had survived far worse. Of those assembled on the plain below, few would even seek shelter. They were a staunch, battle-hardened lot. What did they have to fear from the rain? As Laszlo watched them from the hillside, their howls reached him, spoke to him: songs of great deeds, foes slain and despoiled ground sanctified; dirges for the fallen, warriors mourned and honored for their sacrifice on behalf of Gaia.

Too many had fallen—too many Garou, brave and true. And still the Wyrm writhed and spawned, spreading taint, corruption, defilement—its excrement, sign of its passing. But no matter the cost, the warriors of Gaia would endure, would prevail. Laszlo had no choice but to believe that. How else could he continue to face the changings of Sister Luna?

Looking away from the plain, he cast his gaze higher up the stark hill that had come to be known as Hegy Konietzko. Laszlo could just make out the dark form of the margrave sitting upon a boulder. He was a Garou disdainful of thrones. The Silver

Fangs, in the years they had controlled the sept, had fashioned a throne room in one of the caverns; the margrave had gone so far as to sit briefly upon the seat when the Lords had first regained the sept, but he had eschewed the place since. He preferred the wind at his face, the craggy mountain beneath his haunches, the world before him. The margrave did not suffer pageantry when Wyrm minions remained to be slain, self-indulgence when the salvation of Mother Gaia required relentless striving. He was hard as stone, unforgiving as the mountains.

Looking again to the plain, Korda Laszlo saw two Garou braving the treacherous path that wound up the boulder-strewn hillside. They came as wolves; keeping to the winding trail was easier that way. The first, Laszlo recognized from their simultaneous years of service to the sept. Nyareso Anna, Summer-Rain, had ascended to the position of Warder after challenging and defeating her predecessor. Anna's dark pelt was crisscrossed with scars and signs of battle-honor. Even in Lupus form, her shoulders were broad, her body compact and powerful.

The second Garou was larger, more lightly colored, and carried his own scars. He was an outsider come, as the outsiders were in increasing numbers, to speak with the margrave. Laszlo could tell by the set of his jaw that this one was defiant and headstrong. Often this was the type from the other tribes that was drawn to the margrave's call: young and idealistic, full of anger that the war seemed always to be going against the Garou.

As the two drew closer, Anna Summer-Rain stopped and indicated that her companion should continue. Thirty meters farther up the path, Laszlo stepped forward. *"Jó éjszakát, Hans Schlagen Erst. Beszél németül?"* Hans Strikes First cocked his head but did not respond, so Laszlo repeated himself, this time in German rather than Hungarian. "Do you speak German?"

Hans Strikes First nodded this time. There on the hillside he shifted, his legs growing longer and meatier; he rose upright, and his snout receded, giving way to the light-complected features of his Swiss-German man-form. *"Jawohl.* I speak German."

Laszlo ushered him forward. "The margrave will understand you." The margrave, like Laszlo, spoke several human languages flawlessly. Falling in step with the outsider, Laszlo followed a few meters behind as they climbed a bit farther. The path dipped and ran through a short gorge of boulders, then turned sharply to the left. After the bend, the path opened suddenly onto a wide, windswept rockface which was all the more breathtaking after the brief confines of the gorge. Laszlo remembered the instant of disorientation that had gripped him the first time he had climbed this path. The rockface spread out like the surface of Luna herself, and the sky above seemed to stretch into infinity.

He noted with satisfaction how Strikes First started when he noticed the dark figure perched above him on the hillside. Margrave Yuri Konietzko sat tall and straight. His regally silver hair stood out against the dark fur of his cape, beneath which were visible his thick, bare arms and spiked bracers. The recesses of his face were lost in shadow. Occasionally, starlight caught the ivory and begemmed hilt of the sword at his hip.

Perhaps, Laszlo mused, the margrave did not eschew thrones completely; the seat carved by the Silver Fangs was merely too slight for his tastes, for tonight the very mountain itself was his throne as he looked down in mastery at the young visitor.

"My lord Margrave," Laszlo announced in fluent German, "Hans Strikes First, emissary from the Sept of Mountain Springs."

Faced with the grandeur of the mountain and the margrave, Strikes First seemed to have forgotten Laszlo altogether until the words were spoken. Korda Laszlo was used to as much. His role here was to remain unobtrusive, to keep to the shadows, to observe.

"Greetings, Hans Strikes First, and welcome," Konietzko said in equally fluent German. "It has not been so very long since I traveled to the territory of you and yours. Do you bring word from the elders of Mountain Springs?" The margrave spoke quietly; perhaps it was the acoustics of the rockface that created the impression of Konietzko's voice assailing his audience from all directions.

Gazing up into the night, the outsider's defiance seemed lessened; Strikes First himself seemed lessened in the presence of Konietzko—lessened in both stature and confidence.

"My lord Margrave, I am not before you to speak for my sept," Strikes First said, forced consciously to maintain his proud bearing. "I speak of my own voice and my own mind... and of a few like-minded individuals. Not so few, perhaps," he added.

Konietzko, his darkened features a mask of shadows, regarded his guest for a long moment, then: "What words, then, of your own and of these others do you bring?"

Strikes First hesitated. He glanced around, but he, the margrave, and Laszlo were otherwise alone. "We like what you said to our elders," he began slowly but then picked up speed and intensity, as if once he started talking he couldn't stop. "We like what you said about turning back the Weaver and destroying the Wyrm. Our elders talk and talk and talk, trying to soothe the hurt feelings of other tribes, while our young warriors are dying, and the Weaver is encroaching farther on our territory, and the Black Spirals grow more numerous every day, it seems." Strikes First finished, and his words drifted away into the night.

"I am pleased that my views are well-received," Konietzko said, "but the journey from Switzerland is very long that you should have made it to tell me this."

Strikes First stretched his neck as if his collar were too tight; he glanced around again, reluctant to continue, though certainly he'd had hundreds of miles to choose his words. "The elders..." he said, then hesitated. "They say..."

"What do the elders say?" Konietzko asked, his voice neutral, neither condemning nor lending support.

"They say...some of them, since your embassy to our sept... that you are a demagogue, a tyrant, that you seek power and control for yourself, that you are not to be trusted. They say that you would not merely protect Garou territory but cull the humans, bring about a second Impergium." He seemed almost embarrassed by the aspersions he reported.

"And what do you say, Hans Strikes First?"

"I...I've already told you," he said, taken aback by the question. "I disagree with the elders. As does my pack...and others, friends, from our sept and others. The elders twist your words. We know that the human destruction of the Wyld must be stopped, but that needn't mean enslaving them."

Laszlo observed the unfolding conversation with interest. He could foresee already where it would go. Hans Strikes First was not the first idealistic malcontent to seek out the Sept of the Night Sky; nor was he the first cub to wade far too deeply into the great sea of politics.

"You bring me arguments for and against what I have said," Konietzko stated. "I know these arguments. Is this what brings you so far?"

Strikes First tried to hide his agitation. He clearly had hoped that the margrave would say first what the younger Garou had himself come to say, but such was not to be. With admirable resolve—and no small amount of unease and resignation— Strikes First got to his point: "I...and those I have spoken with... we believe that the Sept of Mountain Springs is no longer best served by the decisions of the elders. I plan to challenge Guy Houndstooth, our leader."

The words hung heavy in the alpine sky. The distant storm was now not quite so distant. Its rumblings were more distinct, and the flashes of lightning partially illuminated the hillside and the plain below. Konietzko's gray-silver mane shone in the electric night, but his face, his expression, his mood, remained ever inscrutable.

"Normally," the margrave said, "I might be informed, as a courtesy, after a transfer in leadership had taken place."

Having steeled his courage to say what he had, Strikes First was unprepared for the flatness of Konietzko's response. The margrave's cool reception completely undid him; he tried to offer explanation but could not form complete sentences, instead babbling, as if he were not the native German-speaker upon the rockface.

"Ah, but you do not wish merely to inform me," Konietzko said, finding meaning amidst his guest's roiling consternation. "You wish some type of aid from me, some form of support." Strikes First nodded, ashamed but also relieved that he needn't voice the entirety of his plan. He would not be free so easily, however. "What support would you have, Hans Strikes First?"

Much to his credit, Strikes First quickly regained his composure and struck the posture of a proud supplicant—but supplicant nonetheless. "I would have whatever support you are willing to give, my lord Margrave. Anything you could teach me that would make my victory more certain."

"*More* certain," Konietzko said. "An interesting choice of words. If you wish to be more certain, then you are not certain at all. Let me see if I understand what you mean. You are certain that you can best Guy Houndstooth in a challenge of combat, for he is old, while you are young and strong. You may even be correct. If you are, then he, as the challenged, would never choose combat. You are less certain that you could defeat him at gamecraft, and so you would like some fetish or word of advice that will assure your victory. As for a contest of wills, you are not certain at all, for Houndstooth is old and wise, and he is master of the rage within his breast. And what payment should I expect for my aid in all of this uncertainty?"

"I would see that the sept followed your will," Strikes First insisted. "You would have additional soldiers against Weaver and Wyrm. Your reach would extend far to the west, as well as here."

Margrave Konietzko sighed. "The affairs of the Sept of Mountain Springs are her own. It is not my place to choose her leader. You told me that you did not believe the aspersions cast upon me by your elders, yet you come here asking me to fulfill their prophecies regarding me. No! Silence while I speak, cub." Strikes First, who had thought to interrupt, closed his mouth and was silent. Konietzko, maintaining his sudden intensity but not raising his voice, continued. "Do you not see the offense in this? Do you share the doubts of your elders? You must, to ask me to become their tyrant! Do you think I won this sept by trickery? Do you think these scars I wear are badges of *gamecraft*?" Konietzko spat the word contemptuously. He rose to his feet, towering over Strikes First. As if in reply, the leading edge of the storm erupted above and around them. A flash of lightning illuminated the margrave's mane, his fierce eyes, the gems upon his sword hilt. Thunder echoed among their ribs. A smattering of large, forceful raindrops splattered against stone and Garou alike. And then the storm struck in earnest, sheets of rain pelting the mountainside, wind tearing at the exposed individuals.

Strikes First instinctively took a step back, as did Laszlo, from the margrave's kindled rage. Konietzko breathed deeply of the storm, but gave no sign of inconvenience. "I do not, however, take offense," he said finally, after a few drenching moments. "I know that offering insult was not your intent. You did not travel so far for that."

"Thank you, my lord Margrave," Strikes First said, clearly relieved. "It was not my intent. I would never...I did not..." His words trailed away beneath the fury of the storm.

"You speak from your heart," Konietzko said, "and your heart is still young and raw. You are a Child of Gaia, and therefore passionate. What you have spoken here will go no further. The words perish, drowned by the storm. But for your journey, I will not send you away forlorn and empty-handed. I offer you these two things.

"The first is advice: Go back to your sept, Hans Strikes First. Go back and listen to Guy Houndstooth. Though he and I may see the world differently, he is wise beyond his years. Listen to him and learn. But know that the Apocalypse is at hand. The spirits sing of it, and Gaia herself cries out for redemption.

"My second offering is an invitation: You, your packmates, your kin, are always welcome here. If your caern is not threatened, come back, cut your teeth against minions of the Wyrm. We always have need of able warriors, and you will be strengthened by your time among us, a blade tempered by fire. For there will be a final battle, and it will be soon."

Strikes First bowed. The driving rain had already plastered his hair to his head; water ran down his face and dripped from the tip of his nose, from his chin, but he seemed not to notice.

Korda Laszlo watched and marveled. Margrave Konietzko had refused in no uncertain terms what the cub had crossed hundreds of miles to ask, yet Strikes First would leave this hillside thankful, and more admiring of the margrave than ever. Any Garou might have been taken by rage receiving the harsh words spoken by Konietzko, but the margrave had cowed his young visitor and at the same time avoided alienating Strikes First.

Konietzko had struck another blow as well. Though Strikes First's words would not leave the hillside, those which the margrave had spoken would spread—and in doing so would counteract the charges of the elders at the Sept of Mountain Springs. The Children of Gaia, like any of the tribes, was a constituency to be courted, and not without its uses. Papering over differences among the tribes was well and good, as far as it went—but in the end, Guy Houndstooth was not warrior born; he was not the leader to give direction to the Garou nation. Desperate times demanded firm direction. The younger Garou seemed to intuit and desire this, and therein lay the hope for the future.

As Laszlo led Strikes First back down the winding path, the Shadow Lord was certain that he would see the cub again, along with packmates perhaps. At the margrave's direction, they would combat the Wyrm wherever it dwelt and whenever it bred—so that Gaia might endure.

Chapter 4

The infectious vibrato of Dawntreader's ululation reached Oksana's ears unimpeded once she opened her cabin door, and a dark shape took wing into the night. From within, she had heard Sergiy's wolfsong for hours as he prepared for the hunt. Oksana had been properly educated in the ways of the rites, and she was accustomed to offering an appropriate prayer before commencing a hunt, but never before coming to the Sept of the Dawn had she encountered any Garou who matched Sergiy's whole-hearted zest for the traditions. As he danced around the raging fire, he did not entreat Mother Gaia for a successful hunt; instead, as with breaking the fast, he celebrated her generous bounty. His song was no petition, but an acknowledgement of his place among, his participation with, all of creation.

Perhaps, Oksana thought, this was how the rites were truly meant to be performed: not as a means to an end, but as proclamation of wholeness, wonder, and joy. The power of the howls and the drums tugged at her, calling her forward. She paused, however, long enough to survey the caern.

Many Garou had already joined Dawntreader and danced naked, or mostly so, around the bonfire. Others were gravitating in that direction, picking their way through the rhododendron thicket now that the time of the hunt was drawing close. Mykola Longbow was part of the dance, as were Taras the Gray and Arne Wyrmbane, the Get fosterling. Snap Dragon, in her natural wolf form, rolled on her back and thrashed to the rhythm of the drums. Neither Arkady nor Victor were in evidence. Oksana was not surprised by the Silver Fangs' reticence in the face of Garou from the other tribes; though she hated to admit so, she shared their sentiments.

Time and time alone had allowed her some semblance of ease in dealing with this menagerie that had collected around Dawntreader. Oksana looked again at the wild dance and noted Yuri Clubfoot, one of several metis who served the sept, and numerous Kinfolk, as well. That such as they should take part in the sacred rites would be unthinkable at the sept of her birthing; she suspected the same was true of Arkady's Firebird Sept. Yet Sergiy's unadulterated ebullience and his conviction that all were welcome made aloofness difficult.

Before joining the raucous prayer, Oksana cast about one final glance. She saw no one who seemed to take undue notice of her emerging from her cabin, none who might have noticed the departure of the dark spirit bird from her quarters. One of the doves that frequented the Penumbral spring might well have noticed the coming and going of the stormcrow, but in any case, Oksana could justify the presence of the messenger if the need arose: Was not an informed advisor better able to offer counsel, and how else should she remain abreast of goings-on beyond the sept? Sergiy would trust her; he *did* trust her.

As she approached the firepit, Oksana was one among many, Garou and Kinfolk alike, forming a ring about the dancers. Dawntreader appeared larger than usual in the golden-flashing light of the fire. He carried no weapon and wore only a vest of white, arctic fur—proof of his far-rangings before establishment of this sept.

Oksana, on the other hand, wore a woolen tunic girded by a belt, and leather leggings and boots. Her hair was still held by the cord and amethyst. The blade at her side was steel, not silver. The pounding of the drums reverberated in her chest, shook her heart with each blow. Mingled strains of howling rose and fell, scattering like smoke and light into the night.

Gradually, those Kinfolk who danced sifted toward the outer ring around the fire, while more and more Garou joined the circling entourage. One after another, human forms dropped away as the wolfsong called more primal urges to the fore. Firelight glimmered from fangs and claws. The howls took on added depth and fervor as Lupine throats became more numerous and the assemblage raised their faces and voices to the heavens.

Sister Luna's eyes were closed tonight, but the Garou strove that she still might hear their song.

Mountain-like in their midst was Dawntreader, his platinum hair reflecting the red flames, whipping hither and yon as he danced. Though still wearing his man-form, his voice was as rich and strong as any. Oksana offered her howl to the sept; the many songs entwined one among another, forming a vibrant chorus to Gaia and the hunt. Oksana removed her belt and held it aloft. The belt was a gift from her elder and fashioned from skin carved by his hand from his thigh—a gift born of unwavering loyalty to the tribe, she presented it now for the Mother's blessing.

Oksana's feet carried her into the dance. The bodies, brushing together as they swirled around the fire, radiated heat and hunger. The howl led Oksana forward, the belt held above her head, as she and her brethren became one in thought and purpose and deed. She was distracted momentarily by the sight of Arkady on the outer edge of the ring. His armor of detachment was not yet pierced, and his expression suggested that he had hoped to seek Mother Gaia's favor in a more private, *civilized* manner. Oksana managed a brief scowl, but then she was past him, and the dance and the howlsong again possessed her. She re-clasped the belt around her waist as she felt the change beginning.

She was Garou, and all that entailed. Woman-form was one face of many, just as Luna wore many faces, and Gaia progressed through the rich panoply of the seasons. Oksana's limbs and trunk grew longer, more heavily muscled. Around her, Garou shifted into all variations between man-form and wolf. Her clothing, attuned to her change, was replaced by a thick mat of gray-speckled black fur; breasts were subsumed by enormous masses of muscle on her chest, sides, and abdomen.

The drumming and the collective howl rose to an intensity almost beyond bearing. Flaming brands settled within the bonfire, and showers of sparks and embers danced toward the heavens. Oksana's movements changed, her center of gravity shifting as her thighs grew as thick as before her torso had been. She was completely covered with dark fur now; only her heirloom belt remained unchanged, stretching to accommodate her increasing bulk.

Still, she continued to shift. Her skull stretched and thickened, her jaws growing more massive and frighteningly powerful. Her arms grew longer to match the length of her legs, and she dropped to all fours. Ears laid back atop her head, she raised her face and voice heavenward, bellowing her hunger, causing the night to echo her predatory intent. She was not alone in her song.

As members of the sect whirled and snarled and danced, she found herself beside the most massive of the Garou collected there, a great platinum dire wolf, at least a meter taller than her at the shoulders. There was a wolf of pure white, too, pawing at the outer edges of the ring, chafing to run, to hunt. Dawntreader, the great flaxen beast, raised his head a final time as all the hunters in unison sounded their prayer, and with the crescendo the bonfire collapsed in a tremendous spray of red and gold. And like the sparks and the embers, the Garou in a kinetic burst shot out into the waiting night.

Chapter 5

For the second time in as many nights, Yaroslav slipped through the back door of the old man's cottage, pausing only momentarily at the uneasy bleating of a goat in the back pen. Satisfied that his presence had not triggered a more widespread and revealing restlessness among the livestock of the village, Yaroslav entered the house, pulling the door securely to behind him.

Absent was the odor of smoldering wormwood, and in its place—or perhaps masking it—was an even stronger, more pronounced, pungent smell that was quite familiar to Yaroslav. He walked past the cookstove with its simmering pot of borscht. One did not deal with peasants in the Ukraine without growing accustomed to the ripe scent of cooking beets and cabbage.

The old man, again, was in the front room in his straight-backed chair. Again, he was carving. But tonight he was not alone; two other men were in the room. One, bald with small, round spectacles, sat in a sagging chair with torn upholstery. The other, taller man with spiky dark hair stood near a corner; his arms were crossed against his chest, but his left hand was obviously missing, replaced by a wooden facsimile.

"You left the girl in the woods," the old man said, not bothering to look up at Yaroslav.

"Yes." Yaroslav instinctively sniffed at the two newcomers. The stench of cabbage covered their scents almost as completely as it did last night's residue of wormwood.

The old man was busy at his carving. Another goat, Yaroslav saw. Then he noticed that the pile of figurines had been removed from beneath the old man's chair. Tonight the tiny creatures, no taller than ten centimeters each, were lined around the room:

along the mantel, across the back of the dilapidated upholstered chair, behind the ceramic oven, across the threshold of the doorway in which Yaroslav stood. They led one another in a parade with neither beginning nor end, an uninterrupted caprine ring.

"Good," the old man said. "I feared you'd be fool enough to bring her here before I was prepared."

"Watch your tongue, grandfather. Or has your addled mind already forgotten our conversation last night?"

The old man laughed at that, and the two other men joined in belatedly, uncomfortably. "This is Yaroslav Vovkovych," the old man said, cutting into the wood that would soon be yet another goat. A shaving fell to the floor, onto the blanket, with many others. "My friends, Yaroslav Vovkovych, you may call Marcus and Nicoli." He waved his knife at the standing and then the sitting man. "And my friends," the old man added, "be respectful of Pan Vovkovych, for you are not worthy to lick the dung from his boots—or so he would have us believe." The renewed, hesitant laughter from Marcus and Nicoli did nothing to ease the tension that bathed the room far more consistently than did the flickering light from the kerosene lamp.

The old man made several more cuts on the wooden goat he held, then sat back and inspected it. Satisfied, he closed his knife and turned to the window sill behind him, where he placed the final figurine.

"Are you ready, then?" Yaroslav asked. He willed himself to remain patient; to do otherwise would be to play into the hands of this lowborn cur.

"Ready? Not quite," the old man said. "Your little wolfling girl can wait. Go get Ihor from the pen," he told Yaroslav. "It was he who welcomed you upon your arrival."

"Welcomed…?" And then Yaroslav remembered the nervous goat out back. Ire flushed his face. "I am not here to play your goatherd, old man. Mock me again and it will be not the blood of the Fang lordling that stains the ground, but yours."

"Do I try you so, Yaroslav Vovkovych?" The old man smiled his twisted, yellow smile. "Marcus," he said, "go get Ihor."

Marcus, who had been smiling along with the old man, grew surly, his mocking grin draining away in favor of a scowl. But he did as he was told. A few moments later, he led the worried goat in the back door, past Yaroslav, and into the front room. The beast, though agitated, stepped carefully over the wooden miniatures on the threshold.

"You may have the honor, Marcus," the old man said.

Almost at once, as Yaroslav looked on, Marcus raised his left arm and crashed his wooden hand down upon the base of the goat's skull. The creature staggered and collapsed onto the blanket.

"What we undertake tonight requires sustenance," the old man said, the warped smile still creasing his craggy features.

Yaroslav did not attempt to conceal his disdain for these pitiful beings who consumed captive beasts rather than hunting wild prey. They were so far beneath him as to make comparison unthinkable, yet thus was his lot, his calling, to consort amongst the lowborn, the despicable, the Wyrm-tainted. For Gaia and tribe. Even such as these, the old man, the two would-be murderers, had their uses. Though surely, it seemed, a Silver Fang lordling deserved a cleaner, more honorable death than what these fiends would bring him. The elders had deemed otherwise, however, and Yaroslav carried out their will.

Yaroslav waited for the old man to produce a knife, so that he and the two executioners could slaughter the beast. Let them get on with it if they must, Yaroslav thought, so that he could play his part and be gone. But the feast was not to be what he expected.

"Good Ihor," the old man said, stroking the beard of the stunned goat. And then the old man unhinged his jaw. His wrinkled skin stretched over the bones of his face, pulled tight by his gaping maw.

Nicoli and Marcus looked on eagerly, hungrily. The old man scowled at them and, with great difficulty because of his wandering jaw, spoke: "I see...how you watch...Ihor. Stop! Remember...this is food...not a brothel!" The sound he made next might have been laughter, but Yaroslav was hard-pressed to tell for certain.

Not wanting to witness this abomination, still Yaroslav looked on, transfixed, as the old man slipped his mouth over the goat's head: over the nose, the eyes, the ears and horns. His neck bulged like a serpent's as he ingested the beast. Ihor seemed to overcome his shock slightly at this point, but managed only a few spirited kicks before Marcus and Nicoli rushed to aid the old man. They took hold of the goat roughly, and each snapped two of its legs near the body, so there was no chance of the poor creature leaping to its feet. It writhed ineffectually, like a fish out of water, as the old man engulfed its neck. Next he folded the broken front legs, and stretched his maw even wider to consume them.

Finally, Yaroslav looked away. He was far from squeamish, but such unbridled corruption disgusted him a thousand-fold more than the pervasive stink of cabbage and beets. He thought of the girl cowering in the woods where he had left her—but his attention was distracted by the scraping of hooves on the floor behind him.

For Gaia and tribe, he told himself, over and over again. *For Gaia and tribe.*

Chapter 6

Oksana loped through the forest, following a scent but half-heartedly. For the first few minutes after the culmination of the prayer, she had sought sign of prey as fervently as any of the Garou. She'd even caught the same trail as Dawntreader; she'd seen him and a few others rushing ahead at one point, but with her gradual return to a more rational mindset, she had slackened her pace, and by now Sergiy would have far outdistanced her. This was as she wanted it. Let the Children of Gaia range ahead in pursuit of the hunt; Oksana, daughter of shadows, sought different prey. Or so she suspected, judging by the tidings Stormcrow had brought to her.

With Sister Luna hiding her face, the forest was dark, and surprisingly quiet considering the number of Garou prowling about. They had scattered widely. Many hunted silently, but occasionally a howl went up, a scent discovered, and others answered the call, converging, taking up the chase of some soon-to-be-sacrificial beast. Among the human villages, many stories would seed tonight and take root. Milk would sour, babes would cry for their mothers' breasts, and men would wake with more gray in their hair than when they'd laid down their heads to sleep. The pious would cross themselves and pray to the Virgin for intercession; the less pious would search the depths of a bottle for courage or blissful oblivion.

Oksana still held the shape of the ancient dire wolf. Her woman-form would have been less useful in the night forest, unaware of the myriad sounds and smells that caused her wolfen ears to prick up, and her nostrils constantly to test the wind. So it was that she was not caught off guard by the sound of motion above her—not even the quiet fall of a paltry stick from the canopy escaped her. She lashed around in the darkness, and her mighty Hispo jaws snapped shut, obliterating the twig.

"It is fortunate that I did not drop a stone," said the dark figure in the tree. "You might have broken a tooth."

Oksana bared her teeth and snarled. She did not recognize the voice; he spoke Russian, not Ukrainian as would most members of her adopted sept. She suspected this was one of the individuals Stormcrow had told her of, and whom she was expecting to encounter. "Your name?" she growled in the guttural tongue of the Garou—her mouth and tongue would not easily wrap themselves around the human speech at this point.

"I will climb down and speak with you," he said, "if you promise not to do to my leg what you did to the twig."

"Your name?" she growled again, unsure if he'd understood her. Was he Garou, or merely a simple-minded fool who courted death?

"Vladimir," he said, answering at once both of her questions. "Known as the White among my brethren at the Sept of the Brooding Sky."

Vladimir Bily. The White. Oksana knew of him; she knew of the long, ragged scar that lined his face, and that, when he wore his wolf-forms, showed only as a streak of white on his otherwise black fur. She knew also other tales about him, and other names he was called, though not in his presence: Child Marrow was one of these, for his rumored favorite meal.

"Climb down," she said.

He did so, pausing as a new series of howls from the hunt reached their ears. Satisfied that the Garou calls were not close by, he continued down and stood beside Oksana. Seeing his scar, and sure of his identity, she assumed woman-form to facilitate conversation. After so many years, the shift came easily to her, second nature, like stretching after a long sleep.

"Listen carefully, Oksana Yahnivna. We have little time," Vladimir said more abruptly than Oksana would have preferred, but she was merely beta to a leader of one of the lesser tribes, while Bily served Eduard Sun-Curser of the Shadow Lords. "I have a request to make of you," Vladimir said, though his tone belied the nature of his "request." Bily did not seek a favor; he expected obedience.

"What would you have?" Oksana asked. Her chief loyalty was, of course, to the tribe—but that did not necessarily mean to the Sun-Curser, nor to his underling.

Vladimir hesitated. Another howl. Closer this time. Oksana recognized the call of Mykola Longbow to the north; she had drawn blood. And from the south came a reply, and a second: Arne Wyrmbane and Yuri Clubfoot. It was odd, Oksana thought, that the Get fosterling had taken to the metis, Clubfoot. But they were both savage, relentless warriors. Perhaps that was the bond between them. They were two of the Garou from the Sept of the Dawn whom Oksana would *least* like to have stumble upon her tête-à-tête with Bily. And their howls were growing closer.

"There is a village, ten, maybe eleven kilometers to the west, in the pass—"

"I know it."

"Victor Svorenko must go there tonight. A woman is there who will betray him."

"A woman," Oksana repeated.

"Yes. One of the Kin of this sept."

Oksana's eyes narrowed. She tried to recall whom she had not seen at the bonfire—for to have made it to that particular village, a human would have needed to leave earlier. She tried also to remember which Kinfolk Svorenko had spent any time with since his arrival. The answer was not difficult. "Liudmila," Oksana said.

Vladimir cocked his head and raised an eyebrow. "Very good, Oksana Yahnivna," he said with a thin smile. "Yes, Liudmila waits to betray the Fang lordling. You must send him there. For his own good, of course. He'll want to deal with the treacherous bitch personally."

"But do you not know that Svorenko's cousin, Lord Arkady, is here?" Oksana asked innocently. "They will be hunting together tonight. Where young Svorenko goes, so will go Lord Arkady."

Vladimir's lingering smile faded. "Do it." He did not like

being questioned. He liked less the ever-nearing huntsongs of Arne Wyrmbane and Yuri Clubfoot. "Do your duty," he said, absently running a finger along the scar that ran from his left temple to his jaw; whether the gesture was remembrance on his part of duty rendered, or an implied threat to Oksana should she fail to carry out hers, she did not know.

"Of course I will do my duty," Oksana said.

Vladimir Bily nodded curtly and then slipped away into the darkness.

By the time Wyrmbane and Clubfoot passed by a few minutes later, Oksana was again the legendary dire wolf. She had pawed and stomped about; Vladimir had concealed his scent well, but she wanted to ensure that no trace remained. Squatting to piss at the base of the tree he'd climbed from, Oksana considered that as her statement on Vladimir's and Sun-Curser's conceptions of her duty.

She fell in behind Wyrmbane and Clubfoot, following easily the two hulking man-wolves. Neither had paused to acknowledge her with more than a brief grunt—not with Longbow's call so close to the north. When Oksana reached the prostrate stag pierced by an arrow in its neck and with another plunged deep in its breast, Mykola, Arne, and Yuri were tearing, snout-first, at the creature's vitals. Its eyes stared glassily into the distance. Longbow would already have thanked the spirit of the deer; the Children were sticklers for such rites.

Respectful of Oksana's station, the others made room for her to join them. She rooted about in the innards until she found the liver, then ripped the luscious organ free with a twist of her powerful jaws. It was gone all too soon, in a quick gulp, but Oksana felt the strength of Gaia entering her body as the camaraderie of the hunt bathed the four Garou, as surely as had the sunrise warmed her that morning.

As advisor to the grand elder, Oksana could have claimed a larger portion of the kill, but she edged away, allowing the younger Garou to have their fill. She lay down nearby and contented herself with the smell of fresh venison, and with working at the small chunks of liver caught between her teeth. Still, her mouth watered at the mere proximity of steaming entrails.

It was not for Garou, she thought, to live on *vyshnyas* alone.

Yuri Clubfoot was the next to finish. He limped toward Oksana—he always limped—stretching luxuriously as he came. He spread his huge man-wolf body beside her on the ground, rubbing his belly gently and emitting a low, warbling growl of pleasure from the back of his throat. "Those antlers will be a good trophy for Longbow. Maybe a good fetish," Clubfoot spoke in Garou-tongue as he rolled onto his back.

Oksana growled assent. "And the hide, too," she said. "Maybe Alla will prepare it for her. Alla is the best at tanning."

Clubfoot let out a puzzled yip. "Alla? No, Liudmila is the best tanner of the Kinfolk, by far."

"I have seen Alla's hides," Oksana insisted. "They are very nice."

Clubfoot rolled onto his side and propped himself up on an elbow. "They are nice," he agreed, "but Liudmila's are much better." Arne was wandering over to join them now, while Mykola dressed what remained of the carcass. Clubfoot turned to his friend for vindication. "Oksana Yahnivna thinks that Alla is the best tanner of the Kinfolk."

Arne Wyrmbane shook his massive head vigorously. "No. Not Alla. Liudmila."

Oksana flipped her chin to the side—what for a human might be a shrug. She chose her words carefully; the Garou-tongue was not so subtle as human-speech. She wished to skirt certain facts without resorting to the telling of untruths. "Where is Liudmila?" she asked. "Someone told me she had left the caern before. I did not see her at the fire."

"Hm?" Yuri yipped again. "She must have been there."

"I think she left before," Oksana asked. "To the west. I hope she is well."

"She would not have missed the bonfire," Yuri said.

"Maybe Victor would know," Arne said. Yuri glared at him.

"I think," Oksana said, "that Victor and Liudmila are... friends?"

Arne snickered, but was quickly silenced by a growl from Yuri. "She would not have missed the bonfire," Clubfoot repeated.

"So you say," Arne snapped. "But saying does not make it so." Yuri growled again.

"Do not trouble yourselves," Oksana said. "It is not important."

"Not important," Yuri echoed, satisfied.

"If something is wrong with Liudmila, then it is important," said Arne, unconvinced. "You said yourself, Yuri, that she would not have missed the bonfire. Maybe she did because something is wrong."

"I did not mean to upset you so," Oksana said. "Look, here is Mykola, finished dressing her kill. Let us return to the caern."

"You return to the caern," Arne snarled. "I will find Victor. Victor will know if something is wrong with Liudmila."

"But Victor is out hunting," Oksana said, concerned. "You will never find him in the woods at night. Talk to him in the morning back at the caern." She paused, then added: "Where it is safe."

"Ha!" Arne scoffed. "You go back to the caern where it is *safe*. Clubfoot can limp back with you, as well. I will find Victor, and we will find Liudmila."

"You make the stones seem smart!" Yuri barked.

"Come back with us," Oksana urged, but Arne Wyrmbane had already turned and, with a defiant howl, plunged headlong into the forest.

The three remaining Garou had indeed started back to the caern when they heard the howl from the opposite direction— the howl of a hunter, of prey within sight. At once, they reversed their track and answered the call with howls of their own.

Mykola Longbow, with the carcass of the deer slung across her shoulders, quickly fell behind, and Yuri Clubfoot had no hope of prevailing in a foot race; there was ample reason he was not named Yuri Fleet-of-Foot. And so Oksana streaked ahead of the other two. A moment before, she'd been guiding Yuri and Arne through a conversation of her choosing, the Get fosterling running off on an errand that she had not quite suggested—but now the huntsong rang in her ears and her blood ran hot. She wove her way among trees and thickets of brambles, adding her song to the tenor of the night.

She recognized the hunt call, of course. They all did. Dawntreader had marked his prey, and now, as Oksana drew closer, the grand elder's howl changed from that of pursuit to combat.

Combat? What in these mountains would dare turn and offer battle to the force of nature that was Dawntreader? Oksana knew soon enough. Snarls and the wet sound of claws rending flesh came to her through one final thicket barrier. She crashed through with abandon, heedless of the branches and briars that ripped at her thick coat, and an instant later came face to face with Dawntreader, his bloody claws raised to the darkness above, gore and flesh trailing from his mouth which was open in a roar of triumph. At his feet lay a huge brown bear, its throat torn so completely open that the head seemed almost a separate creature from the massive sprawling body.

Oksana looked on this sight of magnificent carnage in awe—and ever so slowly a distant notion, a nagging doubt, forced its way stealthily into her thoughts: What might this ineffable beast that was Dawntreader do if he discovered treachery amidst those upon whom he'd bestowed trust?

Chapter 7

The flames, stoked modestly now that the hunt was waning and Garou again gathered around the fire, lazily caressed the brands that lay across the red-orange coals. Song, laughter, facetiously contentious snarls, and other sounds of full-bellied merriment filled the caern and drifted into the night. Grease dripped into the fire, hissing and popping, from the skewers of those who wished their meat cooked. Such activity barely registered in the thoughts of Oksana Yahnivna Maslov, however. Unlike many of the others, she had not killed tonight—not in the context of the hunt, at least.

As she stood, staring at the play of light and shadow amidst the coals, the radiant warmth of the fire warmed the front of her woman-form until it was hot to the touch. Her back was cold. Around the firepit, the flames cast dancing shadows of Garou, flickering, distorted images of Gaia's chosen.

Many of the members of the Sept of the Dawn had returned to the caern. Many, but not all. Sergiy was away, undoubtedly attending to the skin and accoutrements of the mighty bear he had brought down. Such a magnificent kill portended spiritual favor; much of a great beast—pelt, teeth, bones, heart—if properly sanctified, might become fetishes of great mystical power. Dawntreader would be among the spirits, honoring them, enticing them, for hours. At the least, he would pause at dawn: to celebrate, as he did each morning, the bounty of Gaia; and to oversee the Rite of Accomplishment planned for young Victor Svorenko.

Victor and his cousin, Lord Arkady, were conspicuous in their absence at the moment. No one was concerned. Several Garou had not yet returned from the hunt, Arne Wyrmbane also among them. And though most of the Kinfolk of the sept were present, one particular woman was not: Liudmila, of whom Vladimir Child Marrow had spoken.

The scarred Shadow Lord had said that the Kinswoman waited to betray Victor Svorenko, but Oksana knew better than to take Bily at his word. Oksana had been aware of the burgeoning relationship between Victor and Liudmila—there was little that transpired within the sept of which she was unaware—and in days past, the stormcrow messenger had told Oksana of the Garou, her tribesman, who had surreptitiously met with Liudmila on several occasions. Stormcrow had relayed, too, the approach of another Shadow Lord—Bily, the scarred one, Child Marrow—into the territory of the Sept of the Dawn, and what his presence might engender.

Tonight's encounter with Bily had confirmed in Oksana's mind what she had already suspected. The Shadow Lord who had gained the confidence of Liudmila might well have thought that he was instigating a plot to destroy Victor Svorenko, scion of the Silver Fangs. But Bily's arrival, and more specifically the timing of it, put the match to that paper-thin lie. Why would Eduard Sun-Curser, secure in his Sept of the Brooding Sky, and whose bidding Bily did, care about young Svorenko? Was the cub's klaive so deadly? Hardly.

But Lord Arkady, leader of the Firebird Sept had ventured far from Moscow and into what Sun-Curser considered his territory, the Ukraine. A provincial, over-reaching Garou might take umbrage at that—and there were certainly rumors of worse regarding the Sun-Curser. Arkady, despite rumors of his own Wyrm-taint, had fought admirably, even inspiringly, since his return to Russia. His hand, along with that of his Queen of the House of the Crescent Moon, Tamara Tvarivich, was one of those that had struck telling blows in the war against the Hag— while Sun-Curser had built walls against her, and burrowed into the earth like Cousin Mole, rather than confront danger.

Sun-Curser inspired only fear and distrust among the Garou. And Bily was his master's servant. Vladimir knew of Arkady's presence here, Oksana was sure. The scarred one did not care about young Svorenko, except inasmuch as the cub could lead Arkady to his doom. But how? How did the seeming sacrifice of the Shadow Lord courting Liudmila assure the destruction of Arkady, as must be Bily's purpose?

Oksana had performed the favor that Child Marrow had asked. She could hardly refuse and kindle the disfavor of the Sun-Curser, but loyalty among the tribe was hardly monolithic. There were many stormcrows and many masters, all of whom sought to please Grandfather Thunder in their own fashion.

"Are you hungry, Oksana Yahnivna?" a voice asked her from not far away. Oksana's focus shifted from the entrancing flames to Gennady, who stood beside her. He held a strip of venison, still sizzling from the fire. "Have you eaten?" he asked her.

In the past, Oksana had seen Gennady as a towering reddish-brown man-wolf; she had seen him hunt and kill and revel in the blood of his prey. At those times he was fully Garou, approaching the magnitude of spirit that Dawntreader demonstrated daily. Yet at times like this, facing his man-from, his *boy*-form, she saw a tentative, unsure cub, anxious to please. How could Sergiy suffer this whelp? she wondered. Why did Dawntreader encourage such *weakness*?

She snatched the strip of venison from the boy's hand and tore the meat between her teeth, ignoring the searing grease that burned her fingers and mouth. "Leave me be," she said. And Gennady, without protest, without challenge, backed away.

Where was Dawntreader? she wondered. If he were truly strong, he would not sap the spirit of his people with foolish talk of service and humility. If he were truly strong, she thought, he would not trust an advisor of the Shadow Lords who was bound to betray him.

Oksana spat the bite of meat into the fire and threw the rest of the strip onto the ground. She stalked into the darkness, away from the fire. When the sounds of revelry were but a distant echo, she stopped and removed the leather cord that bound her hair.

For a long moment, she held the attached amethyst in her hand and tried to stare into the dark, cloudy recesses of the gem. Then she knelt and placed it on a rock. She took another rock and smashed it down onto the amethyst. As the rock struck, a geyser of violet steam erupted from the gem, obscuring almost completely the sound of impact. The steam blossomed into a gaseous swirling mist of purple and indigo.

Oksana stepped back. When the mist cleared, standing amidst the broken shards of amethyst was a tiny hatchling, a young, newly formed raven, blinking at the crisp air of the open night. Oksana held out her hand, and with only a second's hesitation, the spirit bird stretched its wings and flew to her, landing in her palm. Oksana raised the raven to her lips; she kissed it gently, and then whispered to it. A moment later, the creature was aloft, flying free into the night.

Chapter 8

The girl did not hear Yaroslav approach through the darkened forest. He was already at her side before she realized he was near and started suddenly. "You have the jar?" he asked. She nodded. She was shivering.

Liudmila was a dark beauty. Yaroslav was not surprised that the Fang lordling had grown enamored of her silky hair, brown doe eyes, and pleasing body. Svorenko's attentions to the girl reflected the hypocrisy of his tribe: She was not Fang Kin; were she to take with child, even should it prove to be Garou, the Fangs would never accept the bastard cub as one of their own. But Svorenko was willing enough to pleasure himself with her.

Perhaps, Yaroslav thought, he would take the girl for his own after all of this was over. Svorenko would certainly have no further need of her. Yaroslav had witnessed their coupling: From the shadows, he'd watched the lordling grasp her generous hips and mount her; Sister Luna's light had glimmered against Liudmila's pale, swaying breasts. And Yaroslav had known lust and envy and hatred. Perhaps he would keep her.

"I thought I heard wings," she said, as he led her toward the village.

"This is the forest. Of course there are birds."

"No," she said. "These wings were close. They kept coming back."

Yaroslav ignored her. As the outermost huts came into view, he was more concerned with remaining undetected. There were not likely to be peasants out at this time of night; by the same token, however, should someone see him and the girl, two travelers, strangers to the village, would stand out noticeably. But the village was quiet, and they reached the old man's house without incident.

Inside amidst the stink of cabbage and beets, both Marcus Wooden Hand and Nicoli the Bald had stripped to the waist. They stood on opposite sides of the room; even so, they were merely a few meters apart. Both of their torsos were crisscrossed with countless deep scars; some appeared to be long, raking claw marks, while others were single, snake-like lines that wove their way seemingly across kilometers of flesh. Perhaps they formed some type of runes or symbols; their placement did not strike Yaroslav as random, yet he was at a loss to interpret any meaning.

The old man still occupied his chair above the blanket. He leered at Liudmila, to the exclusion of acknowledging Yaroslav. Atop the ceramic stove rested certain paraphernalia which the old man had gathered: a kettle, whistling and emitting foul-smelling steam; two clear shot glasses; and a flat, time-faded, tile icon adorned with the aspect of the supplicant Virgin.

Young Liudmila glanced worriedly at Yaroslav; she stayed close at his side. Precisely how old the girl was he didn't know. Eighteen or nineteen, perhaps? She was Kin to the Children, and familiar with many ways of the Garou—but the preparations taking place in this house among the old man and his accomplices, the rites that were about to transpire, were different, sinister, darker than the ways to which she was accustomed.

Yaroslav had spoken slippery, convincing words to her. He liked to think that it was his personal charm that she had found irresistible, but he knew the sway that a Garou could hold over lesser beings, even human Kin. He'd come upon her alone, far enough from the caern not to gather notice, and though she'd received his initial overtures hesitantly, he was Garou, and her Garou Kin had been good to her. Flattery, intimidation, and truthful-sounding lies were all tools of the shadows, and Yaroslav had wielded them skillfully. By the time she had agreed not to alert the guardians of the caern of his presence, the girl was his.

Now, and not for the first time this night, she was experiencing second thoughts about what she had agreed to. Her thin, delicate fingers took hold of Yaroslav's forearm. He liked the feeling of that: the sense of protectorate, of ownership.

"She has the jar?" the old man asked Yaroslav, though his rheumy gaze was fixed on Liudmila. The old man's breathing grew labored, his inhalations causing a wheezing sound deep in his chest that was strangely harmonious with the whistling kettle. Whereas before he'd feigned indifference, now an unmistakable palsy seized his hands; a rivulet of brown spittle ran down his chin.

"She does," Yaroslav said. Leading her within the ring of carved goats, he held out a hand. Liudmila reluctantly reached into a fold of her woolen wrap.

"No!" The old man shot to his feet with an unbridled urgency that surprised Yaroslav and alarmed Liudmila. The old man pushed Yaroslav's hand away and smiled, exaggeratedly, a *tour de force* of dingy teeth and blackened gums. "*Her* hand. Must be poured by her hand."

Liudmila, wide-eyed with trepidation, held the small, kiln-hardened jar. The old man had regained his calm, but now the girl's hand began to tremble uncontrollably. Marcus and Nicoli stood watching like graven idols.

"Careful," said the old man, "careful," as he collected the tile icon from atop the oven. The tile was hot, steaming, but the old man picked it up and held it firmly in his bare hands. Yaroslav noticed the odor of singed flesh competing with the powerful aroma of borscht and the foul kettle-steam, which he recognized as the sharp, unmistakable tang of urine.

"Pour it," the old man said, staring at the jar in Liudmila's hand. "Pour." He held the tile before her, flat against his palm.

The girl glanced at Yaroslav, and he nodded. Hesitantly, she unstopped the jar and poured a thick, milky liquid onto the tile. The old man favored her with his gap-toothed, yellow and black smile. Quickly, he moved to the ceramic oven. He tilted the icon so that the liquid ran down, across the image of the Virgin, and into the kettle.

The old man set his face squarely in the spout of steam and breathed deeply. He closed his eyes. "Yes. Seed of lordling joined with piss of moon and stars. The deed is all but done."

As the words were spoken, Yaroslav suddenly smelled blood—fresh blood. He looked around hurriedly. To his shock, both Marcus and Nicoli were bleeding. Some of the scars on Wooden Hand's chest had opened and were weeping reddish-black blood; the bleeding scars were in the shape of a full, round circle. Nicoli the Bald's scars had answered the rite, as well. The outline of a large, five-pointed star on his chest hemorrhaged corrupted blood.

The old man, meanwhile, was lifting the kettle in his bare hands. His flesh sizzled and smoked, but he was unconcerned. He poured, filling the two small glasses, then returned the kettle to its perch. That done, he went back to Yaroslav and Liudmila. The two bleeding observers made no move toward the glasses, which were apparently meant for them.

Neither of the glasses, Yaroslav knew, were meant for him. His job was to provide for the old man what elements his dark rites required. That, Yaroslav had done. The murder of pompous Svorenko was up to these abominable creatures.

"Well done," the old man said. Then, in the next instant, his carving knife was in his black, ruined hand. Like lightning, he drew the blade across Liudmila's throat. Yaroslav knocked the blade away—but too late. Liudmila's hand went to her throat and came away fluttering, wet with blood. Her shock turned to disbelief, and quickly to panic.

"Yaroslav?" Her voice was weak, tremulous. Then again: "*Yaroslav?*" More emphatically, begging him to save her.

But she bled freely, as if her wound answered the nearby moon and stars—except whereas those supernal bodies wept red-black streams, her wound was a river of blood, spurting to the time of her heartbeat. Yaroslav could do nothing but feel the pressure of her fingers, clawing their way down his chest as she slumped to the floor.

He fought down his rage. He wanted so badly to surrender to the blood-thirsty man-wolf, to rend these unholy creatures limb from limb—but he must remember his place. His duty was not yet done. His tormentors had not yet played their assigned role. Even so, he struggled mightily to maintain control. These fiends were allies of the moment, he told himself. And she was merely human, cast-off plaything of a Silver Fang lordling. But she lay staring at him, still pleading with her eyes, from the floor, as her blood soaked into the blanket and wood carvings. Yaroslav had to look away, to abandon her in her final moments. His body quaked with fury.

"Hurry!" the old man said, shoving past Yaroslav and returning quickly with a wide, shallow pan. He lifted Liudmila's head by the hair and positioned the pan beneath her, so as to catch her blood. She hadn't the strength to resist him.

Yaroslav raised his eyes to the smoke- and water-stained ceiling. "You never said you needed *her* blood for the rite," he snarled through clenched teeth.

"Not for the rite," the old man said. Yaroslav could almost *hear* the cruel, yellowed sneer. "For the borscht. One grows so tired of cabbage."

It was more than Yaroslav could take. He squeezed fists that began to grow larger. He gnashed his transforming teeth with such force that he drew blood within his mouth. His hackles were raised and his vision red with rage, but before he completely changed, the tiny house erupted into chaos.

The window behind the old man's chair exploded in a spray of shattered glass and wooden fragments of obliterated shutter. An instant later, the bolted front door and the back door exploded inward as well. Within the space of a single heartbeat, a blur of fangs and claws splattered blood across the walls and ceiling of the suddenly very crowded room. The snarling, mottled, white beast through the window landed on the old man, tore one of his arms fully off, and sank fangs deep into the base of his neck.

The Garou that burst through the front door was a blur of pure white coat and blazing silver claws. The first swipe tore away Nicoli's face, the second rent a terrible chasm through the five-pointed star on his chest. Yaroslav's change complete, he hesitated nonetheless, unsure which side to attack; the sudden burst of violence checked his own rage for the moment, and the raw fury of the pure white Garou was an awe-inspiring spectacle to behold, indeed. Yaroslav's indecision stole from him the immediate matter of choice.

A third Garou, towering above the other two, if that were possible, crashed into the room from the kitchen and knocked Yaroslav aside. Marcus had just managed to raise his wooden hand in response to the attacks. The third Garou clamped its mouth down on Marcus's elbow, lifted him off his feet, and, whipping its head violently, shook him like a helpless rag doll until the wooden hand, severed, clattered to the floor.

Jostled to the side, Yaroslav stumbled—over Liudmila. Managing to shift his attention partially from the magnificent white beast, he dropped to the floor and pulled the girl's unresisting body to the side, through patches of her own blood and that of the conspirators. Perhaps five seconds had passed since the Garou's attack commenced.

The battle would have been decided had these been mere humans under attack. But the old man, bleating now at the loss of his second arm, sprouted three new appendages from his trunk. Each ended not in a hand but a jagged razor. As one, they tore into the mottled Garou, whom Yaroslav now recognized as the pompous lordling, Victor Svorenko.

The silver-clawed, pure white Garou, Lord Arkady, had problems as well. Nicoli was blinded and screaming in agony. His mangled form could no longer contain the Wyrm-taint and corruption of his soul, and his blood, red-black before as it seeped from his chest, now ran all dark. It sprayed, a fountain of burning decay, and all that it touched sputtered and steamed and blackened: wall, furniture, and Garou alike. Arkady's snarls of pain joined the din of combat.

The largest of the three Garou, Arne Wyrmbane, fosterling of the Get of Fenris, was known to Yaroslav, as well. Wyrmbane, having discovered this particular flavor of corruption was not to his taste, flung Marcus against the far wall and began spitting and pawing at his own mouth. The flesh he'd torn from the enemy's body was rotted and crawling with maggots and parasites. Wyrmbane shook his head forcefully and gagged. Meanwhile, a torrent of flying and stinging insects poured from the stump of Marcus's ruined arm, quickly filling the room.

At almost the same time, the tiny wooden goats, which were arranged in a ring about the room and had watched silently all that had transpired tonight, began to change before Yaroslav's eyes. They grew tall and insubstantial, no longer wooden figurines but phantasms of swirling shadow. They went first after raging Svorenko, who contested against their master. For every arm the Garou ripped from the old man's body, another one or two snaked back to take its place. And the serrated razors at the end of each were hitting their marks. Svorenko's blood ran red and true. The shades grasped at his wounds, prying at lacerated flesh. Svorenko slashed savagely at the old man's hydra-like limbs, but he was losing ground. More of the shadow beings were entangling the Garou's legs and arms, blocking his vision, and inexorably pulling him to the floor. The old man roared in triumph; one after another, stubby caprine horns forced their way through the skin of his forehead.

Nearby, though Marcus now seemed little more than an empty, desiccated husk lying limp on the floor, Wyrmbane, too, was struggling. The insects that swarmed about him were too small and insubstantial for him to fight. His brute strength and massive claws were nothing to them. With each swath he cut through the swarm, thousands more insects instantly filled the space. The shades were targeting him now also. They wrapped en masse around his bulging forearms and biceps; they snaked around him and drew tight about his neck. Soon his mounting rage worked against him, as he snapped and swung futilely. In his anger and frustration, the shades unbalanced him, and with one of his mighty but utterly useless swipes, he went crashing to the floor.

Arkady, his own fur smoldering and flesh burnt from the ichorous spray of Nicoli's corrosive black blood, was not unaware of the plight of his comrades—nor was he panicked. The only Garou standing, he had more room to maneuver now. He drew his grand klaive and with one broad swing sliced Nicoli's head from his shoulders. A black spray erupted from the wildly flailing torso, but Arkady lithely sidestepped it—and in the same motion caught the kerosene lantern on the tip of his klaive, flinging the light onto Marcus's shriveled body.

On impact, the lantern and the shell of a body burst into flame with a great *whoosh* that singed Yaroslav's fur. Instantaneously the swarm of insects, which had been blinding and voraciously biting at the Garou, turned and tried to go back to the body. The flames scorched them by the thousands in a cacophony of satisfying pops and sizzles.

Now Arkady turned to face the old man and his plethora of gyrating, razor-tipped arms and his stubby goat horns—and all the shades, sensing which foe was the greatest threat, flocked to the smoldering pure-blood Garou. His klaive sliced through them, a dozen at a time, but they seemed to reform as quickly as Arkady could cut them down.

The old man cackled as he continued to slash at the fallen Svorenko. Arne Wyrmbane tried to catch his breath after being choked by maggots, insects, and ethereal shades. The phantoms, meanwhile, forced Arkady back toward the fire, which had spread to the adjacent wall and was rapidly climbing upward.

Mid-cackle, the old man came up short, as his head flew from his body. For several seconds, his arms continued to lash out, more slowly each strike, and then his headless corpse toppled over onto the blood-slick floor. As one, the shades assailing Arkady jerked upright, then suddenly seemed to take on weight, each falling to the floor. But what hit the floor were hundreds upon hundreds of wood-shavings. Those that landed on the blanket soaked up puddles of blood. Many simply fed the fire, which continued to spread and was now threatening to engulf the house.

Arkady turned from his non-existent foes. Svorenko and Wyrmbane slowly climbed to their feet. And there, standing over the decapitated body of the foul creature that had been the old man, and staring at his own bloody claws, was Yaroslav. A menacing growl began low in the throat of Victor Svorenko and was taken up by the other two, as smoke filled the fiery, blood-drenched room, and the three furious Garou closed in on the Shadow Lord.

Chapter 9

Footsteps and pawsteps sounded off the smooth stone as Korda Laszlo led the two emissaries along the corridor. It was a night for emissaries, he thought. Only a matter of hours had passed since the margrave had completed his audience with Hans Strikes First. Laszlo had seen to it that the young Child of Gaia had been accepted around a cookfire where there was meat to spare; not by accident, another tribesman of Strikes First was a member of that particular pack, so the cub was able to see that not only were his kind welcome at the Sept of the Night Sky, but some were taking advantage of the invitation already.

The two emissaries following Laszlo currently were not so easily led in greater affairs. They pursued definite agendas and came not as audacious whelps but elders previously tested by battle and blood, experience and loss. But there the similarities between the pair ended. That two Garou so different should come together in this place was nigh miraculous; Margrave Konietzko was the one who had worked the impossible and shown them their common ground.

The audience chamber when the three reached it was empty; the margrave had not yet arrived. Red coals resting in a brazier took the chill from the air. Wisps of gray smoke drifted lazily upward and into a small shaft cut into the stone ceiling. Tapestries depicting Shadow Lord history, skillfully woven but not ostentatious, adorned the walls: Here Alexandru ThunderRage stepped into the Umbra; there Septumus Dio rent the body of a Roman proconsul; the most recent scene showed Boris Thunderstrike ascendant over Heart-of-Fury of the Silver Fangs, reclaiming the Sept of the Night Sky for the Shadow Lords. Noticeably absent was any representation of Margrave

Yuri Konietzko. A number of carved wooden stools stood against the walls.

"The margrave will be with you shortly," Laszlo said. He had sent word to Konietzko's family quarters. The margrave spent little enough time with his wife—only what was required for intercourse, so that more Garou might be born—and no time with his children, except those who exhibited the gift. No lingering good-byes would keep him from the emissaries and from his duty.

The first emissary, Helena Slow-to-Anger, accepted Laszlo's statement impassively. She had been a guest of the sept for several days already and was in no hurry. She was a tall, wiry woman, thin but strong as steel, with sun-baked olive skin and severely short hair. Her eyebrows, like her, were thin and dark. In the recent past, Kelonoke Wildhair had come to Hungary to meet with the margrave, but presently Slow-to-Anger was here in her stead—chosen perhaps specifically to deal with the other emissary who had just arrived, Swift-as-the-River.

Laszlo suspected that it was not the margrave's absence but rather the mountain over their heads, tons of rock and earth, that agitated Swift-as-the-River. The lupus Garou paced slowly back and forth, the nails of his paws clacking against the floor; his hackles were partially raised. Laszlo had offered food— Swift-as-the-River had traveled far from the south—but the Red Talon had growled that he would hunt for himself when he grew hungry. He paid no attention to Helena, and she little to him. But they were in the same room, for a common purpose— that in itself engendered unlikely, if precarious, hope.

His presence no longer required, Laszlo left them. He slipped through the hewn passageways with a familiarity born from years of repetition. A hand pressed against a particular stone, indistinguishable from those surrounding it, revealed an unseen door which swung silently open and then closed, also silently, after his passing. This passage was narrow and completely dark, but Laszlo knew his way well enough. A few more acute turns and he was in place. The spy-hole was already open, prepared in advance so that the sliding plate would not alert Swift-as-the-River's sensitive ears. Laszlo peered through the form of Septumus Dio; there was no hole in the tapestry, but the special weave was such that the fabric appeared more substantial from the front than from the back. With darkness behind him and the dim lighting of the audience chamber, Laszlo would go undetected, and if need arose, he could rejoin those in the room in but seconds.

From his place of secret observation, Laszlo watched as Swift-as-the-River continued to pace, and Helena tried to ignore his unease. The audience chamber had not been selected specifically to bother the Talon; rather, the storm still raged outside, and decorum seemed to dictate that the host should provide such shelter as was available. No words passed between the two Garou, only alternating glances, when each thought the other was not aware.

Swift-as-the-River was the first to hear the footsteps, the methodical click of boot heels against stone. The Talon's ears pricked up and he ceased pacing; seconds later Laszlo and Helena understood the reason.

The margrave strode purposefully into the room, fur cape billowing behind him, sword comfortably at his hip. He spoke a formal greeting to Helena in Greek, to Swift-as-the-River in Serbo-Croatian. By previous agreement, there was no shifting of shapes. The Red Talon did not deign to assume a more manlike visage, nor did he appreciate for those who preferred manform to match him as Lupus, as if they needed to "compensate" for him in that manner. And so communication was strained at times, laborious at best, but alliances were a stone wall constructed from blocks of accommodation, and the minor stone of eccentricity was often more easily placed than the boulder of far-reaching principle.

"You are returned," Konietzko said without preamble. The Talon preferred directness, as did Helena, as did the margrave. "What did you find?" He spoke slowly in Serbo-Croatian, so that Helena might follow. She knew enough of that human-tongue to get by—one reason Kelonoke had sent her—while Swift-as-the-River understood no Greek and would speak no human-tongue.

Instead, he growled and snarled, sounds that held no

meaning to a human but among the Garou were a natural, well-formed language. "The river does not come back," he said. "Fish, otter, fox—they all die. Water flows but the poison stays." "And what of the humans?" Konietzko asked.

"They know better than the others not to drink from the river—but the humans, they die too."

Laszlo recognized deep satisfaction in that last of what the Talon said. If the Shadow Lord didn't know better, he would have thought that Swift-as-the-River's snarl possessed an element of a smile, as well.

"The water sickens them?" Konietzko asked.

"The water," Swift-as-the-River nodded. "That kills them too."

Too. Laszlo didn't need to guess at the Talon's meaning. Since the dam-burst that had flooded the rivers Somes and Tisza with thousands of cubic meters of cyanide-contaminated water, life along their banks had withered and died: vegetation; animals that ate the plants or fish, or that lived in or drank from the rivers; humans who depended upon the water for life. What villages remained were like ghost towns, largely depopulated. If humans went missing, or even if entire village populations were massacred, there would not likely be anyone to take note for quite some while. And with the rampant political instability in the region, who was to say for certain from whence violence came?

"We must be cautious," Helena Slow-to-Anger said, also sensing the Talon's meaning clearly enough. "Humans are not all creatures of the Wyrm."

"Where the humans are, the Wyrm breeds," Swift-as-the-River said.

"Yes," Helena agreed, "but we must root out the fomori, and destroy the Banes and their pits. The humans we can...persuade, influence."

"No humans, no Wyrm."

"That is not true, and you know it," Helena challenged the Talon.

Swift-as-the-River's hackles, which had smoothed, now raised full. He snarled—not a phrase of the Garou-tongue, but clearly a warning of the lupus. Helena did not match his anger. The margrave waited patiently. The Talon eased his stance slightly. "No humans, less Wyrm," he conceded at last.

While this point of tentative agreement took firmer hold, Konietzko methodically retrieved one of the three-legged stools from beside the wall. He situated himself near the brazier. "As we pursue the destruction of Wyrm-minions, undoubtedly... accidents will occur from time to time. Humans who might not have been tainted will become unfortunate victims." Swift-as-the-River snorted; Helena frowned and folded her arms. "While the humans are embroiled in their own affairs, I see no harm in this. But," he added, running his fingers through his silver beard, "we must take care. The humans will not take notice of us if we do not give them reason to. There is wisdom is Helena Slow-to-Anger's words. She speaks with the voice of Kelonoke Wildhair, whose determination and vision you admired, did you not, Swift-as-the-River?"

The Talon snorted again, as Helena looked marginally satisfied.

"Do not mistake me," the margrave said. "There will be more blood. The fighting is far from done. But the caern your pack recovered in Kosovo, Swift-as-the-River—was the desecration there of human hands? No, I thought not. We must take care to remain focused upon the most dire threat. There will be time enough to deal with the humans once that is taken care of."

Helena was not in complete agreement. "Did you encounter any more of these..." she paused, searching for a word in what was not her primary language, "...these *different* humans?"

Swift-as-the-River stared hard at her. "We did," he growled. "Very few. They seemed like the other humans...except they saw us. They did not run and scream."

"And they showed signs of having...powers—that humans shouldn't?" Helena asked.

"Yes," Swift-as-the-River said. "But they too are dead. No humans, no Wyrm."

"Those that my people encountered did not smell of Wyrm-taint," Helena said.

Swift-as-the-River cocked his head. "Did not smell of the Wyrm, but had to be."

"They are humans," Konietzko said, "and therefore individually of little threat to us. But perhaps your Talon war-pack leaders could tread more lightly for a time. Simply to assure that too many eyes do not turn our way."

"You spoke before," Helena said to the margrave, "of broadening our efforts."

"We have lost many caerns," Swift-as-the-River said warily, "and many Talons trying to reclaim them. How much more can we do?"

"The Talons have indeed fought valiantly," Konietzko said. "As have the Furies, as have the Shadow Lords. And we have made progress, our three tribes, all across the Balkans. Yet, still, certain areas remain beyond our reach, choked full of Wyrm-beasts: parts of Kosovo and Serbia, even along the Tisza in Hungary. Our people have all sacrificed much, Swift-as-the-River. Perhaps where three tribes have made more progress than one, four or five could accomplish greater feats still."

"But the others are busy with their squabbles and human politicking," Swift-as-the-River said. "They are not wolves but men."

"Would you not once have said the same of the Shadow Lords, and of the Furies?" Konietzko asked. "Have we not proven worthy allies?"

"Not the same," Swift-as-the-River grumbled. "The others are not worthy to share meat with the Talons. We die while they turn a blind eye to humans and to the Wyrm."

Konietzko nodded. "Then let us discuss, my friend, how to convince the others to become worthy. And afterward, we will add the information you bring to our maps of the Tisza basin."

Swift-as-the-River finally sat back onto his haunches. Helena retrieved a stool for herself. In his spy place, Laszlo had no such comfort, but he possessed the will and the patience of his tribe.

Chapter 10

Smoke from the rapidly spreading fire burned Yaroslav's eyes as he warily shifted his position and tried to keep all three of the other Garou in sight. They were growling menacingly, seemingly unimpressed by the decapitated corpse of the old man, whom Yaroslav had felled when they had proven unable to do so. Probably stirring contention was the tiny fact that Yaroslav had been conspiring with the foul Wyrm minions; Fangs and Fenrir were always so inflexible in such matters.

For whatever good it might do against such overwhelming odds, Yaroslav called on the strength of Luna to protect him from harm; the Mad Sister was ever-present, though her face might be turned away. Even so, the Shadow Lord had time only to flinch as Arkady swung his klaive.

The flat of the blade slammed down upon the ceramic oven and shattered the two shot glasses, which miraculously had survived the brief but bloody melee. Another flick of Arkady's blade, and the whistling kettle crashed to the floor, spilling its malodorous mixture of urine, semen, and Gaia-only-knew what else.

In the corner of the room that had been the first to catch fire, plaster and flaming timbers were falling to the floor. Yaroslav wondered if he was the only one who noticed that the house was burning down around, and *over*, them—as Arkady brandished the klaive at him.

Yaroslav did his best to focus on the elder Fang. The two fosterlings might be more fierce, but they would follow Arkady's lead. If Yaroslav were going to survive this night, he had to gain the alpha's confidence—or at least his forbearance. Knowing that Arkady wouldn't be so easy to convince as was poor, dead

Liudmila, Yaroslav sought the wisdom of his ancestors to guide his words. He took a deep breath. "We should leave this death-trap now that the enemy is destroyed," he said with as much swagger as he could muster.

He could no longer hear their growling for the roar of the flames. Wyrmbane circled slightly to Yaroslav's rear. His skin crawled at the thought of the Get behind him—death could come quickly from that direction—but Arkady was the one that mattered; his yea or nay would tell the tale. "You are aware," Yaroslav said, risking a bit of condescension to mask his mounting concern, "that this place is on fire?"

Arkady said nothing, didn't lower his silver blade. Yaroslav tried to ignore Svorenko edging closer, and Wyrmbane, *back there*, somewhere. Larger chunks of ceiling began to crash to the floor, adding billowing clouds of plaster dust to the thickening smoke.

"Hell with you," Yaroslav said at last. He started to step past Arkady, toward where the door had been before it was ripped off its hinges. "I'm not going to burn up just because you—"

The flat of Arkady's blade slapped against Yaroslav's chest. He flinched again, recoiling from the threat of silver.

"To the forest," Arkady said. His gaze bore into Yaroslav. "And don't try to escape us. We're not yet done with you."

Yaroslav was not overly comforted by Arkady's tone, but at least they were getting out of the inferno. Yaroslav didn't like his chances of slipping away from the other three Garou, but at the very least, the relocation would give him a few more minutes to think.

Once the decision was made, the Garou shot out of the burning cottage. They were little more than gray and white flashes through the darkness. Even so, the alarmed villagers, who had come as soon as they'd noticed flames licking out of the old man's home, sensed the presence of predatory forces beyond their ken. Many ran screaming from terrors imprecisely defined to them. None clearly saw the lupine visitors to the village, but from that moment forward, the total destruction of the old man's house was assured. No one would try to save it, or its inhabitant; no one would so much as venture near, until cleansing flame and the light of day had exorcised the evil within.

"He killed Liudmila. He should die!" Victor Svorenko, pacing in the darkness, urged Lord Arkady. Arne Wyrmbane growled his agreement.

Yaroslav did not attempt to argue the point. If they'd been listening before they burst into the house, then they would know that he did not kill the girl—not intentionally, not directly. If they had not been listening, then nothing he said would likely persuade them, least of all the two fosterlings. The minutes crept by, and dawn grew closer.

Arkady sat on the slope of a hillock, his chin resting on the pommel of his klaive, the point of which was perched in a crevice of the rocky ground. He listened to his kinsman's rant, but the elder Fang said nothing, and his gaze never left Yaroslav.

"He killed her," Svorenko insisted. "Who knows what other corruption their dark rite would have led to if we hadn't destroyed the others?" Victor's lesser injuries had healed over already, but his white, mottled coat was still marred by numerous wounds from the Wyrm creature that had hidden behind the face of the old man.

As the young Fang stalked back and forth, and Wyrmbane licked his own wounds, Yaroslav remained calm. He willed himself back to his man-form. If this confrontation went the way of combat, he was lost before he began, so assuming his least imposing shape seemed desirable. Human speech, with its vagaries and ambiguities, might also prove useful.

"We should kill him before he does more harm," Svorenko said. Certain words carried enormous weight, great emphasis, when spoken in the Garou-tongue: *kill, harm.*

Finally Arkady rose from his seat. He lifted his klaive—to make use of it, or to sheath it? Yaroslav wondered. Svorenko ceased his pacing and watched his elder cousin. Wyrmbane, too, turned from his wounds to observe the great Silver Fang lord, alpha of the Firebird Sept.

"You were conspiring with minions of the Wyrm," Arkady

man-wolf stated. "Why should we not kill you?" *Wyrm. Kill.*

"Because the appearance of corruption and corruption are not one and the same, Lord Arkady." Yaroslav bowed slightly. He was risking much. Rumors of Wyrm-taint had trailed Arkady for years, as doggedly as his own tail. Once an exile from Russia, now banished from the North American protectorate of King Jonas Albrecht, Arkady had nonetheless fought valiantly in the war against the Hag.

"You know me," Arkady was pleased by recognition, by the weight of his renown. He paused briefly, shifting from singed but still magnificent, white Crinos to man-form. He was tall and regal despite the burns that marred his person. "But I am at a disadvantage as to whom I address."

Yaroslav bowed again, more deeply and formally this time, until fully genuflected. "But a humble servant of Gaia, Yaroslav Ivanovych Neyizhsalo."

"And from what sept do you hail?"

"I travel my own way," Yaroslav said, his head still lowered, "aiding the warriors of Gaia however I may." It was true—as far as it went. Yaroslav had served many septs and many alphas in his day; he saw no need to mention the name of Eduard Sun-Curser, for whom Arkady held a fierce, and public, antipathy.

Arkady considered the reply momentarily, then: "So tell me, Yaroslav Ivanovych, how it was that you were aiding the warriors of Gaia by consorting with the Wyrm?"

Yaroslav ignored the derisive snort from Svorenko and formulated an answer carefully. Such a delicate matter—and carrying potentially dire consequences. Yaroslav considered mentioning Arkady's own past—the aspersions cast against him, undoubtedly baseless—but decided against it. The noble and powerful never appreciated their own circumstances being compared to those of more common creatures, so Yaroslav quickly decided to dwell on his own situation. For the second time tonight, he called on the wisdom of his ancestors to guide his tongue—lest he should join them in the spirit realm permanently.

"It is true, Lord Arkady, that I came to be in consort with creatures of the Wyrm," Yaroslav conceded. Arne Wyrmbane bared his fangs, but the Shadow Lord continued: "It is true that I might have attacked the fomori at the village when I first became aware of them, but the Litany instructs us: 'Combat the Wyrm wherever it dwells and whenever it breeds.'"

"You needn't lecture me regarding the Litany," Arkady said.

"Forgive me." Yaroslav hurried on: "But my hope was that, instead of destroying a few corrupted humans, I could learn of the nest in which the Wyrm was breeding, so that I might alert Dawntreader, as he is rightful protector of this territory."

"You quote the Litany," Svorenko interrupted, "but you ignore where it tells us: 'Respect the territory of another.' Instead of announcing your presence to Dawntreader, you crawled on your belly in the darkness, like the Wyrm-thing that you are."

"I must ask your forbearance and that of Dawntreader, as well," Yaroslav said, actually glad of the accusation, which distracted attention from his creative recitation of events. "But I felt that formal contact with the sept would jeopardize my activities against the Wyrm minions."

"How did you come to be aware of the fomori?" Arkady asked.

The answer fell to Yaroslav like manna from heaven—but, still, he was not yet ready to thank his ancestors, though his debts to them were mounting. "It was the girl who led me to them," he said, and Svorenko's ears instantly pricked up. "Of course, I did not know at first that she was tainted...."

"He lies!" Svorenko roared.

"I must confess to...tender feelings toward her," Yaroslav continued. "I saw her bathing in a stream, where she would come alone occasionally, and I approached her."

"She would have told us," Wyrmbane offered. He seemed slightly confused.

"One would think," Yaroslav agreed. "I even suggested she introduce me into the sept, but she refused. She said there were dark deeds afoot, and that I should stay away from the caern. I thought her words and actions odd, though she was generous enough with her virtues." He ignored a dangerous growl from Svorenko. "So I took to following her, and she led me to the village. I confronted her and convinced her to take me to whomever she was meeting. I told the old man what he wanted to hear, and he took me into his confidence."

"As you are now telling us what we want to hear," Svorenko said.

"He was Wyrm-spawn and unworthy of truth," Yaroslav said. "You are warriors of Gaia."

"What did you learn, then, Yaroslav Ivanovych?" Arkady asked. "What of the Wyrm nest?"

Yaroslav's mind was racing, but he maintained a facade of calm. He had angered Svorenko enough to avoid the impression of pandering, but the Shadow Lord needed hard evidence, something concrete, to fortify his position. He cast the net of his thoughts wide and, ironically, pulled back a morsel of truth that might yet save his life.

"I might have learned more," he said, "had you not attacked and I been forced to defend you." Svorenko groaned and drew his claws, screeching and shedding sparks, across a rockface. But Yaroslav continued undeterred: "It is easier to draw milk from a he-goat than to pry secrets from a Wyrmling, but I heard them speak of an old mine to the west of here. A full day's journey."

Arkady considered that. "A full day's journey," he repeated under his breath, as he studied the early-morning sky.

Yaroslav knew that he had piqued the Silver Fang's interest, pricked the alpha's pride—but was it enough? Did Arkady believe him, or would Svorenko and Wyrmbane get their bloody wish?

"We will go to this Wyrm pit," Arkady said at last. Yaroslav repressed a sigh of relief.

Svorenko was less pleased. "But it is almost sunrise. We should kill this traitor and go back to the caern for my rite."

Wyrmbane seemed not really to have believed that Arkady would seriously consider mercy for a Shadow Lord caught conspiring with fomori. The decision, or perhaps the Get's own confusion, sorely agitated him. He began snorting and raking his claws down an elm sapling, which was soon little more than kindling.

"He should die," Svorenko insisted, growling. "He conspired

with Wyrm-spawn. He killed Liudmila." *Die. Kill.*

"We do not lightly take the life of Garou, Victor," Arkady said with a harsh edge to his voice; his decision was made, his patience at an end. "The final battle draws nearer with every rising and setting of Sister Luna, and we grow weaker fighting amongst ourselves. All of those who are the salvation of Gaia are already born, or have you forgotten the prophecy?" he asked Svorenko. "Yaroslav Neyizhsalo is Garou. The girl was but Kinfolk, and likely tainted at that. Do you not understand this?"

Svorenko hung his head and was silent. Yaroslav felt vindicated; though his mission had failed, he was thankful at least to have survived, and ready to be on his way.

"So we will go to this Wyrm pit," Arkady said again. He turned to Yaroslav: "And you will go with us." Yaroslav's heart dropped into his stomach. "We will fight the Wyrm together. When we return to the caern, Victor, your Rite of Accomplishment will be one of many."

One of many Rites of Accomplishment, Yaroslav thought, or perhaps the rites would be Gatherings for the Departed.

Chapter 11

When the raven had finished whispering in Oksana's ear, she took from her hair the leather cord that had been attached to the amethyst, and made a loop in one end, which she then slipped over the raven's talon. The other end of the thong she tied around the sturdy brace of a wooden shelf that held a small, silver-backed mirror. The spirit bird sat contentedly, blinking in the flickering candle light of the cabin.

"And what does your little featherling tell you?" Vladimir Bily asked.

Oksana was pleased that she didn't start. She had not heard him enter her cabin, had had no idea he was there until he spoke. Perhaps he had just that instant stepped into the physical world. "Is it wise for you to be here?" she asked coolly.

Vladimir the White laughed quietly. "Your spirit guardians will no more catch breath of my presence than you did."

"Underestimate Sergiy Dawntreader at your own peril," Oksana said with a shrug. Though Vladimir was of her tribe, she found strangely heartening the thought of Dawntreader disemboweling and dismembering the Shadow Lord.

"Ah, but it was you who sent an honored guest of your sept to his doom."

Oksana, though in her woman-form, repressed the instinctive urge to bare her teeth to her tribesman. In speaking so plainly of his scheme, Vladimir endangered her—less from threat of being overheard than by destroying her screen of deniability. Last night, he had danced around the actual purpose of his coming, though his meaning had been clear enough to Oksana. But now, how could she hope to face a Truthcatcher and disavow knowledge of Bily's nefarious intent? Assumptions were not knowledge; she could deny them easily enough. But this comment—this trod very close to the line of diplomatic etiquette among the Shadow Lords, a line that Child Marrow would never inadvertently cross.

"Whatever do you mean?" Oksana asked the scarred one. "I merely expressed concern over a girl who was absent from the caern. If pressed," she said in way of warning to him, "I would readily admit that my concern stemmed from the comments of a clandestine visitor, who for some reason did not wish to reveal his presence to the sept. If there is danger, perhaps I should warn the leader of the sept?"

Vladimir laughed again, slyly. "Surely Lord Arkady is able to care for himself."

There it was, then. As if Oksana needed confirmation of her suspicion: Bily's plot, and therefore the Sun-Curser's will, was for the destruction of Arkady. Yet Vladimir danced ever so closely to the line of deniability without *quite* crossing over. Perhaps. Technically, he had merely expressed his confidence in the Silver Fang.

"What *has* your featherling told you?" Vladimir asked again.

She considered putting him off, or lying to him, or coming as absolutely close as she possibly could without *actually* lying—but Oksana decided that the less she tried to manipulate him, the more likely she would be to recognize his attempted manipulations of her. "A certain group of fomori to the west have been destroyed," she said, "by Lord Arkady and the fosterlings, Victor Svorenko and Arne Wyrmbane. And another Garou also: by the name of Neyizhsalo. You might know him?"

"I have made his acquaintance," Bily said coyly.

"The four are now headed west, in search of greater glory."

"And into greater danger?" he asked, mockingly curious.

"Such remains to be seen."

"Indeed it does. Shouldn't you alert the leader of your sept?" Bily asked, feigning concern. "Everyone must be overwrought with anxiety for Lord Fang and the cubs."

"The telling should fall to Arkady," Oksana said. "His deeds, his glory."

"How convenient," Child Marrow smirked.

It was true enough that the entire sept was wondering of the whereabouts of Arkady and the fosterlings. Sunrise, the appointed hour of Svorenko's rite, had come and gone with no sign or word of them. Yuri Clubfoot mentioned something about Liudmila, but the conversation in the forest had not struck him as significant enough to recall in detail. Sergiy had seemed to take their absence in stride. The rite was not tied to Luna's phase; the cubs were hunting with Arkady. They would return when they returned. And all morning, and all day, Oksana had said nothing.

"Who would have thought," Vladimir said, "that a noble Silver Fang, presented with an opportunity for glory, would hurry off recklessly, perhaps even to his doom? And this Neyizhsalo—I hear tell that he is a slippery one. Hearsay. I, of course, do not know him well. I imagine that, found out in some devious plot, he might shift loyalties for convenience's sake."

Oksana listened silently. This was more than merely Bily's pride talking—though certainly he was pompous as any Fang. Still, his reputation for lethal treachery would never have become what it was were he blind to subtlety. No, he wanted Oksana and, through her, other Shadow Lords to know who was responsible for the elimination of Lord Arkady of the House of the Crescent Moon. There was to be no mistaking that the honor garnered within the shadow moot of the tribe belonged to Bily, and to Eduard Sun-Curser. Outsiders might suspect, but the Shadow Lords would *know*.

Everything Vladimir said was to that end, while still he left Oksana just enough—just *barely* enough—room to deny full knowledge, should Dawntreader or any other outsider seek to question her. She could not help but admire Bily's skill. Admiration, however, did little to heighten her regard for his person.

"You'd best leave," she said, her words cold and unequivocal, like a klaive thrust into Bily's chest. "You would not wish to be discovered here," she added, veiling her contempt, if transparently, with the proper amount of deference. Like Child Marrow's revelations, her unstated barbs approached, but did not cross, the line of proper decorum.

Bily smiled in recognition. He moved toward the raven, but ignored the bird. He touched lightly the silver-backed mirror on the shelf, and then, with but a nod to Oksana, he stepped sideways into the spirit world, leaving the cabin as empty as if he'd never been there.

Chapter 12

A full day's journey. Perhaps that was true, Yaroslav thought, for someone who knew where he was going. As it was, Brother Sol had risen, climbed high in the sky, descended toward the west, and finally set altogether—and still the four Garou had not reached any mine.

"He has lied to us," Arne Wyrmbane grumbled periodically. *Lie. Wyrm. Kill.* The Get fosterling was comfortingly predictable.

Still, Yaroslav, too, had grown frustrated as the journey continued to draw on. He had never claimed to know where the damnable mine was nor ever to have been to it, yet with each ridge crested that did not produce a panorama of blasted, marred, gaping earth, he felt the glares of the others' bore into him with increased ferocity—if, from the fosterlings, that was possible.

Late in the afternoon, they had come upon another village. Arkady, a true alpha, had been unwilling to ask directions, so it had fallen to Yaroslav to take human-form and speak with the humans. A gnarled, hen-pecked old villager had said that he remembered a forsaken tin mine, still farther west, while his shrewish wife had called him foolish. He was crazy, she said. There was never any mine, and Yaroslav should go back where he came from. Not exactly brimming with confidence, he had returned to the other Garou; they had taken the couple's quarrel as *his* fault, somehow. He should be accustomed when traveling with Silver Fangs, Yaroslav told himself, to being the perpetual scapegoat. He let the thought pass—after all that had transpired, he did not wish to dwell on goats.

In addition to allowing Yaroslav to be the recipient of considerable scorn and countless aspersions, the journey afforded him time to reflect. As his potential death and dismemberment at the hand of ostensible allies receded into the past, and the prospect of whatever Wyrm-thing they might find lingered ever over the horizon, Yaroslav wondered at his predicament. What were the chances, he asked himself, that Lord Arkady, alpha of the Firebird Sept hundreds of miles away, would be visiting upon the night Yaroslav had set out to accomplish his mission? What, Yaroslav wondered, were the chances that Vladimir Bily did not *know* Arkady's whereabouts when the Shadow Lord had instructed Yaroslav to go forward? The already long odds lengthened considerably when one considered the chance that Arkady, even if he were visiting the Sept of the Dawn, should stumble upon the fomori cabal in the midst of incriminating activities.

Yaroslav was basically accustomed to the animosity of Garou from other, inferior tribes, but he was truly disturbed by the emerging direction of his own thoughts: that his failure was not accidental, that he had been set up, *sacrificed*. If that were the case, then Bily, or someone, had deemed Yaroslav expendable. He was never expected to return from this mission—an ill omen, indeed, for whatever lay before him still.

Perhaps, he considered for the first time, being in the company of two Silver Fang Arhouns and a brutish Get was more fortuitous than he had realized. Regardless, though, knowing Bily and the ruthless lengths to which he regularly, and quite cheerfully, stooped, Yaroslav would not have bet even money on his chances to see another sunrise. He was never meant to return.

A full day's journey. An abandoned mine. Sounded simple enough.

"He has lied to us," Arne Wyrmbane muttered. "We should kill him and go back." *Lie. Wyrm. Kill.* The Get fosterling was comfortingly predictable.

Chapter 13

The candle had melted down to a molten glob on the table. Oksana, in bed, had not noticed the instant when the wick had sunk into the mess and the lone flame had flickered its last. Even in the darkness, reflective red eyes shone amidst the primordial midnight that was the raven.

Oksana was not asleep. Despite having had no sleep the night before during the hunt, and none since, she lay awake, staring at the ceiling. The weave of her blankets seemed particularly rough tonight and itched against her skin. The main culprits keeping sleep at bay, however, were her own thoughts.

Vladimir Bily had left her hours ago, yet his presence lingered in the cabin like an unshakable malaise. Oksana had gone so far as to step into the spirit realm herself, to make sure he truly was gone. She had found no sign of him. Still, sleep seemed distant and alien.

Oksana was no admirer of Silver Fangs in general, nor of Lord Arkady in particular, that she would mourn his passing. The idea stuck in her craw, though, that she should bear witness to Bily's accomplishment—should his scheme play out as he envisioned. Other concerns, more significant than personal animosity, weighed upon her, as well. She owed a certain amount of loyalty to Sergiy Dawntreader and this sept. Not that she shared his fanciful, utopian vision of all Garou living in peace and harmony, but through her service to Dawntreader, she tied the Children of Gaia more firmly to her true masters at the Sept of the Night Sky. The fact that she was not, and had never been, publicly acknowledged as a member of that sept worked to her advantage.

Bily seemed to believe that he and his "acquaintances"

were the only shadow moot of significance, or that Oksana would quietly acquiesce to his plans. Perhaps he assumed that every member of the tribe would welcome the destruction of Arkady at his hands. That was what the stormcrow, last night, had warned Oksana. Her task was to turn the situation to her advantage, to the advantage of her masters, without creating an outright schism among the Shadow Lords. How to do this, she had pondered—and pondered, and pondered more.

The question that Child Marrow had left unanswered amongst his sly boasting, and of which Oksana had no way to learn, was: To what doom had he sent Arkady and the foster-lings? How could he be so sure they would not return?

Finally, she pulled back her blankets and faced unprotected the cold of night. Darkness was her time—as Garou, as Shadow Lord. She made her way to the red eyes of the raven. She unleashed the gaffling; it stepped willingly to her offered hand, and again she whispered to the spirit bird: "One more task I ask of you, Raven, and then you are free to be on your way...." It cocked its head at her instructions, as if curious, but when she finished speaking, it alighted from her hand, taking to wing, and disappeared from the mundane world mere inches shy of striking the ceiling that Oksana had studied so intently.

Chapter 14

"You cannot begin to know the array of matters that demand the margrave's attention," Korda Laszlo said.

The Garou tight on his heels was not dissuaded. "I *know*," Gryffyth SeaFoam said enthusiastically, as if his own point were proven by Laszlo's words. "I must see him resolve dilemmas if I am to compose songs of his grim determination and unerring intellect."

"Must one break open the clock to tell the time?" Laszlo asked.

"If one wishes to observe the genius of the clockmaker, then yes!"

Laszlo sighed. He searched for the appropriate words in the English human-tongue. "You are...tiresome, SeaFoam."

"Ceaseless as the tides, I'm sure you meant." Gryffyth kept at Laszlo's side but was forced to jump out of the way whenever they passed a servant in the narrow stone corridors.

"The margrave cannot possibly see you now," Laszlo said, coming finally to a thick wooden door and stopping.

"And why is that?"

"Because, at this moment, I have no idea where he is."

Gryffyth blinked. "Oh." He glanced over one shoulder and then the other, as if the margrave might be lurking around a corner.

"He was to leave the caern tonight," Laszlo said. "He may already have left."

"Oh," Gryffyth said again. "Well...upon his return will I be able to see him?"

"I will see what I can do."

"I cannot craft great songs without a proud and worthy

subject," Gryffyth said. "Surely he would like for me to do for him what Dagger's-Edge has done for Anatoly Masaryk at the Thunderstrike Sept."

"I am certain," Laszlo assured the Galliard, "that the margrave will accommodate you when he is able."

Gryffyth accepted that, if grudgingly, and ambled away down the corridor. Laszlo opened the wooden door and stepped inside, where Margrave Konietzko awaited, seated at a broad stone table.

"What kept you?" the margrave asked, not altogether patiently.

"Forgive me, my lord Margrave. I was fending off Gryffyth SeaFoam. He thinks to do for you what Dagger's-Edge has done for Anatoly Masaryk. Even if he is half as successful—"

"Hmph," Konietzko scoffed. "He will not be half as successful. I have heard SeaFoam's songs. He doesn't possess half the talent of Dagger's-Edge."

"Still," Laszlo reasoned, "his goodwill could be useful."

"Only should his songs influence Son-of-Moonlight and the restless cubs he leads."

"That is the hope, of course," Laszlo agreed. "SeaFoam wishes to observe as you 'resolve dilemmas,' so he might sing of your 'grim determination and unerring intellect.'"

"Sounds as if he's already written the songs."

"It might be that humoring him slightly will pay significant dividends," Laszlo suggested. "Dagger's-Edge's work *has* raised considerably the renown of Anatoly Masaryk in Russia."

"Masaryk's sword raised against the Hag is what won him renown, and rightfully so," Konietzko snapped. "Not like thrice-damned Sun-Curser, huddling behind his walls and fencing at shadows."

Laszlo bowed and risked a bit of irony: "Your intellect, as always, my lord Margrave, is unerring." There was a long, uncomfortable moment before Konietzko smiled. The margrave was often not of a mood to appreciate irony.

"Then I suppose we're due for some grim determination," he said, his smile turning more calculating. "Summer-Rain's scouts report an outpost of Leeches five leagues north. Send for

SeaFoam. We leave in an hour. He will observe as we burn out the vermin. How do you think he will like the resolution of that dilemma?"

"I can hear the songs already, my lord Margrave." Laszlo bowed again and backed from the room.

Chapter 15

Raven soared high above the mist-shrouded mountains. With Luna away, even his sharp eyes were challenged to pick out details of the Umbral landscape far below. There was little enough to see: a broad expanse of inviting forest, interrupted here and there by rocky outcroppings. None of the Wyrm scars in the immediate vicinity were significant enough to be visible—not from this height, not with the light this poor. It was near one of the Wyrm scars that he would likely find those he sought, but for the moment Raven soared and drew sustenance from the spirit world.

He had been bound for so long. Not that the gem had been torturous or painful—just confining. But now the Garou woman had set him free; he simply need complete one more task for her. A curious thing that she asked of him—but what a tiresome existence it must be: always to be bound to the ground, unable to take flight. No wonder the task she set for him was odd. A small enough price for freedom. Perhaps when Raven tired of flight, he would return to this strange Garou and aid her further—but then Raven's caw echoed like laughter from the trees and mountains far below; he would never tire of flight, of freedom.

Weaving his way through the darkness, his wings caught an updraft and he climbed, higher and higher. The wind lifted his ephemeral body, but also passed through him, seeped into his very being. Such was the spirit world that it infused him with strength and vitality.

Still higher Raven climbed, slowing as he went, until finally his momentum withered to nothing and he paused for the briefest instant, motionless. Then he was diving, picking up speed, faster and faster, as the wind tore across his beak, his eyes, his feathers. One more task to complete for the Garou woman, then freedom.

With the wind screaming past, Raven pierced the Gauntlet that separated the spirit and the mundane. He crossed over with some small wistful bit of longing, but he would be back to his natural world soon enough. He swooped low over the tree-tops and almost at once saw what he wanted.

The bat was flittering near the ground, chasing bugs that bred along a pitted, rocky slope in scattered pools of stagnant water. Raven was silent. His mundane counterparts were hunt-ers of corn and shiny baubles, but he was a creature of spirit; he had learned a trick or two from Falcon and from Owl. And with flashing talons, he put those tricks to his own use.

He smelled blood.

And freedom.

Chapter 16

As the hours of darkness passed, and the four Garou climbed higher and deeper into the Carpathians, and still there was no sign of a mine, Yaroslav Ivanovych Neyizhsalo more and more frequently considered his options. He tried to divine what might happen if they never came upon the mine, which seemed likely; they had followed a rugged track westward from the village where the hen-pecked husband had directed them. Perhaps the shrewish old woman was right, and her husband was crazy. The Garou would continue to wander aimlessly amidst the mountains. This possibility left Yaroslav to contemplate how his newfound "allies" would respond to failure.

The answer was profoundly simple, and profoundly disturbing, as far as the two fosterlings were concerned. Victor Svorenko and Arne Wyrmbane would just as soon tear Yaroslav to shreds and return to their sept as continue searching for some alleged mine. For the moment, they trudged along the mountain track, eyeing Yaroslav suspiciously and angrily at ever-shortening intervals. His reprieve was won only at the order of Arkady. And how long would that last?

It was a question Yaroslav could not answer. Lord Arkady hid his thoughts as skillfully as any Shadow Lord would. Did he grow tired of this doubtful venture? Would his pride and the enticing thought of eviscerating Wyrm creatures soon be overcome by impatience? And if so, what then of Yaroslav's fate?

He could stand and fight the other three—but he might as well rip his own head off, if not for the mere convenience of letting them do it and saving him the trouble. Yaroslav had considered creating or making use of some diversion and slipping away into the darkness, but the others were on guard against that, and though he could mask his scent and hide his trail, Yaroslav could not discount the tracking and hunting—and *killing*—skills of the two Fangs and the Get. The situation was not yet desperate enough, the odds not quite long enough, for him to attempt escape and evasion. Not yet.

Even if he did manage to escape and survive, there remained the question of where he would go next: not back to Bily and the Sun-Curser, that much was certain. But the extended future was a prospect that, without a stroke of good fortune, Yaroslav might never face.

"Many years have passed since this road has seen use," Arkady said, after at least an hour of silence.

Yaroslav had noticed the same thing—he had not, for instance, observed any evidence that heavy machinery, or even thick-treaded automobiles of any sort, had *ever* traveled this route—but he was more concerned at the moment with what lay beneath the words of the Silver Fang. Had Arkady seen enough? Was he prepared now to turn back, to pronounce judgment?

"I say we should be done with this fool's errand," Svorenko voiced his opinion. *Kill.*

Arkady shot his cousin a cold glance. The Silver Fang lord would not tolerate, even by implication, being called a fool. Perhaps young Svorenko's outspokenness was all that prodded Arkady to continue, but continue they did.

Sister Luna again hid her face tonight. Tomorrow night she would peek down at the creatures crawling across Gaia's surface, but for now only the stars watched between the stark branches, still mostly winter-stripped. The rutted track, worn away by wet-season runnels, continued to take them upward, more often climbing steep slopes that led to ridges, themselves merely a respite before the next slope. Yaroslav was as surprised as any when they discovered on one ridge a junction, a crossroad in equal disrepair, and a sign.

The weathered wooden slabs of the sign were crumbling, and whatever paint may have once adorned the Cyrillic letters had long since faded; but carved into the surface of what remained of the sign was one recognizable word: Ólovo. Tin. Such-and-such Tin Mine, or the like, the sign had presumably once read, marking the route to the backwater holding of a state-owned corporation. That the sign was rendered in Russian suggested it originated during the Soviet area, when native Ukrainian would have been frowned upon.

Svorenko told Wyrmbane what the word was, then looked first one way and then the other along the crossroad; the ridge formed a gentle downward slope to the left, while climbing rapidly and steeply to the right. "Which way?" he asked.

The sign might once have pointed the way, by shape or by inscription, but that portion was now rotted away to nothing. Yaroslav looked at the decayed wood on the ground and thought of the fresh shavings on the floor of the old man, the shavings that had soaked up the blood of Liudmila.

"This way," Yaroslav said, pointing to the right. "If ever there are two paths, the hardest and rockiest and steepest is the way."

"Spoken like a true Garou," Arkady said, and they set off up the hill.

This slope was equally as rugged as any they had traversed tonight. The track dwindled away to little more than a barely distinguishable footpath. Yaroslav was now certain that no diesel-powered vehicle had ever climbed to this mine; pack mules, more likely, would have borne supplies up and then ore back down the mountain. But that was all years in the past. Before long, the ridge grew as narrow as it was steep and craggy—treacherous on all accounts. So intent were the Garou on maintaining their footing that they almost missed completely their goal. It was Arne who saved them that embarrassment.

"Look. There," Wyrmbane said.

Yaroslav and the others looked where he pointed. To the right of the path, tucked in a fold of the hillside was a conical crater, maybe twenty meters wide at the rim, with steep rock and earthen walls that converged at the bottom. At that point, a central shaft boring down into the mountain seemed to have been boarded up, but like the sign at the junction below, the boards were moldy and rotting. The black shaft was partially visible through the boards and the piled leaves and earthen tailings that had collected there.

Yaroslav's visions of a vast, man-scarred, desolate landscape, mountainsides torn away as tribute to human short-sightedness was far too grandiose for this abandoned mining concern. Here someone, mostly through the sweat of his brow and backbreaking labor, had tried to pillage Gaia's riches and had either failed or given up. A slight scar remained, a canker that in time would heal; there was injury, yes, and insult, but the human intrusion into this region was more pathetic than damaging. The frail, dying villages, which the young humans fled as soon as they were able; hillside fields once tilled, now left fallow and increasingly reclaimed by the Wyld; this inane gouging of a mine—in time Gaia would cleanse herself of them all.

But the old man had mentioned this place; he had said to summon the others from here: Marcus Wooden Hand, Nicoli the Bald, both ash and ember now, along with the foul old man. So perhaps the wounds were deeper than they appeared; perhaps Black Spiral Dancers had fashioned a hive, or a Bane could lurk beneath the surface—or *nothing*: The old man could have lied, or this could be the wrong place.

Yaroslav tried not to think of that possibility. He hoped they would find some minor Wyrm creature which the Fangs and the Get, their pride and their blood up, could dispatch, and Yaroslav would be their comrade in victory. If there were nothing here, nothing at all, they might well turn their thwarted aggression toward him.

The narrow footpath led down from the ridge to and around the side of the rim farthest from the hill. Beyond that arc of the path, the mountain fell away precipitously. On the opposite side of the crater, the hillside rose as an extension of the crater wall. Before moving closer, Arkady shifted to man-wolf. He stood tall and magnificent, his pure white coat gleaming in the starlight, most of the burns from last night already healed. The others followed suit. Yaroslav felt noticeably overmatched among the three Arhoun warrior-born. He fell in step behind Arkady; even now, the fosterlings weren't willing to risk leaving him in the rear.

The odor of decaying vegetation was strong around the pit, and from a closer vantage there did appear to be rough-hewn steps in the wall of the crater leading down to the shaft. Yaroslav put a hand to the dagger at his belt. Svorenko, behind him, drew his klaive. Maybe this *was* a Black Spiral hive, Yaroslav thought. A *small* hive, he hoped, quick work for brutes like his companions. It wasn't exactly how he preferred to spend his evening, but perhaps if he stuck close to the others and kept his head down...

The steps were on the far side of the crater, at the end of the path after it snaked around the exposed portion of the rim, but Arkady stopped abruptly on the near side, forcing the others to do so as well.

"And what is this?" the Silver Fang lord muttered to himself.

Yaroslav, not tall enough to look over the great white beast's shoulder, peered around him instead. Sprawled across the trail lay a peculiar sight: a furry bat carcass, wings spread wide and undamaged—but its head torn almost completely from its body. Fresh blood pooled on the path, under and beside the remains.

"What is it?" Wyrmbane growled, displeased that those in front of him had stopped suddenly.

Arkady, always alert, now grew hypersensitive. He reached for the hilt of his grand klaive. "I don't like this. It shouldn't be here. Something is not...right. Back up," he said. "Off this path. Now."

That was when the earth erupted. A massive, solid shadow shot from the pit and seemed to blot out the heavens. It kept coming, growing taller, a pillar of flesh and teeth—until it toppled toward the Garou. The four tried to scramble back without falling over one another, but there was no time. Huge as it was, the beast was fast, too. A thick worm-like tentacle extending from the shaft and tipped with gaping maw and razor-sharp, jagged fangs, the thing pounced.

It landed a meter beyond the bat, obliterating the tiny carcass. The very mountain trembled under the impact. Yaroslav and the other Garou were knocked from their feet, and the storm of dust and grit kicked up blinded them—but had they gone just a few steps farther, they would have been crushed as lifeless as the unfortunate bat, or knocked from the rim and off the side of the mountain. Wherever the bat had come from, its misfortune had saved them.

Arkady was the first to recover. He regained his feet and slashed at the beast with his klaive, once and then again and again, powerful blows. Some dug into the thick, segmented flesh; others bounced off harmlessly.

Wyrmbane and Svorenko took only seconds longer to join the fray. There was no room for a second combatant on the path beside Arkady, so the younger Fang and the Get circled wide to either side. Arne, roaring bloody battle rage, jumped to his left. He seemed barely to touch the cliff above the crater as he ricocheted off and landed astride the Thunderwyrm. With flashing claws, he was elbow-deep in blood and meaty gore in seconds.

Svorenko had slower going to the right, where the ground fell away steeply. He made use of the stunted trees that clung tenaciously to the hillside, gripping their gnarled trunks with claws of feet and hands, until he was close enough to plunge his klaive into the hide of the Wyrm-beast.

Yaroslav's response was more measured. Dagger in hand, he backed up Arkady and waited for an opening, but the Silver Fang struck whenever opportunity presented itself. So Yaroslav looked on; he studied the beast amidst the unfolding melee. He had heard tales of Thunderwyrms but never seen one—a state of affairs he would have preferred to maintain. The creature was not without a certain level of reason, he saw. Maybe it was purely instinct, but the feints and lunges with its dagger-fangs suggested strategy. It didn't manage to bite Arkady with the cavernous maw that would have ripped him in half, but the monster's thrusts altered his attacks, wore him down. Increasingly, as Arkady dodged the deadly teeth, the bulk of the Thunderwyrm struck him, visibly battering him. A blow knocked him from his feet again, and the Fang rolled to the side an instant before the creature's jaws crashed shut, churning the earth where he had been.

Amidst the chaos and the dust and the blood, Yaroslav watched for a weakness, a way to defeat the beast—and he could discern none. Not in this type battle of brawn. Quickly he surveyed what he could see of the crater, the path, the hillside....

A landslide! Were there enough loose rocks and rubble

above the pit? But that would bury the Garou as well. Yaroslav
paused, weighed the idea.... No, he would have to be sure to
kill all three of them if he killed any. Otherwise, he might as
well turn tail and run right now—a tempting thought, but if
any of the other Garou survived, surely they would hunt him
down. Frankly, facing an indestructible Wyrm-beast seemed
better odds.

Less so a moment later. Arkady's klaive slashed deeply into
the monster's flesh as the mouth swung past—but the blade
struck at the base of a tooth and held fast. Rather than relin-
quish his klaive, Arkady was lifted from his feet. Reacting to
the pain—or perhaps by design—the Thunderwyrm whipped
its head back the other direction, flinging Arkady through the
air. His blade pulled free and went with him, and he managed
a graceful landing—but thirty meters away.

Meanwhile, Yaroslav stood face to face with the Wyrm. For
a moment, the maw hovered before him, as if the creature had
eyes peering from deep within its gullet. All Yaroslav sensed,
though, was the overwhelming stench of decay which washed
over him. Faced with no other option, he slashed with his
dagger—

—And sliced through thin air. The head whipped away
from him. Until now, the beast had ignored the fosterlings and
the many blows they were landing. With Arkady and his flashing blade of silver gone for the moment, the Thunderwyrm
turned on them. It buckled a portion of its mammoth body, several segments, which snapped and smashed into Svorenko as he
was again stabbing the churned portion of flesh before him. The
bone-snapping blow sent him staggering backward, senseless,
and down the mountainside.

At almost the same instant, the Wyrm-beast doubled back
on itself, its teeth crashing shut on Arne. He roared in pain as
the monster lifted him into the air, and then as he fell—less
one arm and much of his torso. Wyrmbane landed hard. He
growled and twitched spasmodically as his steaming blood
flowed freely and soaked the earth.

Yaroslav's vision started clouding over with red rage. Despite
Arne's insistent threats against him, the Shadow Lord's stomach

constricted at the sight of a Garou savaged so. As Wyrmbane's lifeblood spurted onto the leaves and dirt, Yaroslav's ran hot. He charged forward and plunged his dagger into Wyrm-flesh. The blow was not so deep as what the others had struck, but the Thunderwyrm reacted. It brought its massive body crashing back down to crush Yaroslav—but he had jumped to the side and struck again. The creature rolled to pin him beneath its bulk. Yaroslav was too quick. He rolled this time and swung his dagger, once, twice more.

This time the beast's maw lashed around. Yaroslav ducked. He felt the wind of its passing, smelled the rot. Blood ran between the monster's teeth—Arne Wyrmbane's blood.

Yaroslav felt himself sliding into rage. It fueled his every attack. But as he slashed and dodged, he tried to hold his fury in check. He could not defeat this Wyrm-beast single-handedly. If it were to be destroyed, he must survive to alert others. Giving in to blind rage would merely add his own blood to Wyrmbane's.

As instinct slowly gave way to intellect, Yaroslav cursed himself for attacking the Thunderwyrm. Why had he done it? he wondered. Because a suicidal Get, who would have been happy to take Yaroslav's head, got what he asked for? Where the hell, Yaroslav also wondered suddenly, was Arkady? Had the mighty Silver Fang turned tail and fled?

Diving out of the path of destruction as the Thunderwyrm's jaws crashed down into the earth and carved a huge bite, Yaroslav hazarded a quick glance around. He had seen Arkady land and get to his feet. What had happened to—?

There. There was Lord Arkady. But he was not advancing, not preparing to attack. Instead, he stood with his klaive raised above his head and his *eyes closed*. Yaroslav was so shocked that he was late avoiding the Thunderwyrm's next onslaught. The bloody teeth missed and clattered shut just above his shoulder, but as the beast twisted, its segmented body caught Yaroslav's leg and rolled across it. He wailed in agony as flesh and bone were crushed beneath ton upon ton of Wyrm-beast.

The creature's momentum carried it on, but the damage was done. Yaroslav lay prone before it, unable to dodge. Arkady still did not attack. Yaroslav clutched his dagger, ready for one last feeble attack as the Wyrm struck its killing blow. He noticed across the crater Svorenko climbing, battered and bleeding, back onto the rim. The young Fang would enjoy seeing him die, Yaroslav thought wryly.

And then the inexplicable happened: Nothing.

No killing blow fell. The beast did not clamp down its fearsome teeth on Yaroslav and tear him in two. It did not roll forward and crush him completely. Its front end remained upraised, waiting, but doing...*nothing*.

Yaroslav didn't understand. He could see by Svorenko's expression that the Silver Fang was astonished as well. Shocked or no, Yaroslav wasn't waiting for the Wyrm to come to its senses. He scrabbled backward as well as he could, dragging his mangled leg. Movement was searing agony, but the alternative was certain death, and despite the pain, Yaroslav could feel the crushed bone rejuvenating and knitting itself back together already.

He crawled toward Arne Wyrmbane. The Get's eyes were open, but he stared unseeing. His blood no longer spurted forcefully from the ragged opening in his side and shoulder, but trickled slowly, disinterestedly. With each passing moment, Yaroslav expected the Thunderwyrm to resume its attack, to plunge down toward him, or Svorenko, or Arkady.

But the beast did not attack. It maintained its precarious stance, maw upraised, rear trailing away into the mineshaft. At some point, Yaroslav realized that Svorenko, his befuddlement not lessened in the least, was not watching the Wyrm. Instead, klaive at his side, he stared slack-jawed at Arkady. Yaroslav followed the young Fang's gaze.

Lord Arkady, like the Wyrm-beast, maintained his earlier pose: klaive raised above his head, feet at shoulder-width, eyes closed. But something was different. Arkady's pure coat shone, not starlight-white, but red—red as fire, red as blood. The fiery nimbus encapsulated his body, seemed to radiate from him, from his klaive, as well. Slowly he opened his eyes. Despite the illumination he projected, his pupils were fully dilated, his eyes wide and black, full of wrath. There was something otherworldly to his gaze, something mystical, at the same time ecstatic and pained.

Yaroslav found himself recoiling from that gaze, being thankful that it was not leveled at him. Arkady stared cold fire at the Thunderwyrm. Still holding his klaive aloft with one hand, he lowered the other, slowly, palm toward the ground. As Yaroslav looked on, dumbfounded, the body of the monster buckled and bent. First it lowered its head, and then its whole body, until it lay prostrate on the earth. There, under the light of the stars and the fiery glow of Lord Arkady, the Wyrm-beast bowed down to the Silver Fang.

Had Luna fallen from the heavens Yaroslav could not have been more overwhelmed. To hack to pieces such a foul beast was one thing, but to *command* a creature of the Wyrm…

"What sorcery is this?" Victor Svorenko asked. He made his way cautiously, suspiciously, around the crater rim, around the supplicant Wyrm-beast. "Cousin Arkady?"

The elder Fang moved forward. He lowered his klaive, pointed it toward the creature. The mammoth Thunderwyrm quivered at his approach. "There is a voice within us," Arkady said, his words strangely amplified by the fiery nimbus encompassing him, "that if we but speak, all creation will obey."

If he could have torn his gaze away, Yaroslav would liked to have fled into the night. He tested his leg: The mending continued, but he could not yet support his own weight. Nearby, Arkady radiated power over the beast like Brother Sol radiated warmth, yet something about the transfixing sight filled Yaroslav with dread. He was not alone in his distrust.

"It does not feel…right," Svorenko said, still obstinate in the face of his cousin's glory. "It is not natural."

Arkady's countenance grew brighter. A flash of anger crossed his features. He glared at Svorenko and snarled: "Go then, if you are so weak and simple-minded! I had thought you made of sterner stuff. I see now that I was wrong."

Yaroslav couldn't help but admire how Svorenko turned his back on both the transcendent figure of the fiery Garou and the spectacle of the groveling Wyrm-beast. "Can you walk?" the Fang lordling asked Yaroslav.

He tested his leg again. "I can manage." Any amount of pain was better than remaining there.

"The twisted wiles of the Wyrm are still at work here," Svorenko muttered. He lifted Arne Wyrmbane's limp body and hoisted it to his shoulder.

Arkady seemed to have forgotten them. Svorenko stalked and Yaroslav limped away. The last Yaroslav saw of him, the Silver Fang lord had sheathed his klaive and, still, the Thunderwyrm quaked before him.

But then Yaroslav and Svorenko were around a bend and the crater was out of sight. The Shadow Lord breathed a sigh of relief. Svorenko said nothing; he seemed completely unconcerned with Yaroslav. A few minutes later, when Yaroslav's leg was fully recovered, he slipped away from the trail, and from the Fang lordling, and into the darkness of the forest.

Chapter 17

Silence radiated from the spring, all through the meadow. Even the leaves of the giant willow were still and quiet. All of the caern and all of the sept sensed Dawntreader's mood. Of Garou and Kin, none was more keenly aware of the grand elder's frustration than was Oksana Yahnivna Maslov, she who, alone, sat with him upon the willow roots beneath cowed leaves.

Sergiy lifted his earthenware mug to his lips, but the icy water did little to cheer him. "Death is but a part of life," he said, shaking his head, "yet the cub was in our care. A fosterling." The mug seemed incredibly small in his meaty hands. His flaxen hair lay wild about his shoulders, and his thick arms were tense, as if by the strength of his body he might bring Arne Wyrmbane back. The grand elder wore a bearskin draped over his shoulders, and a string of bear teeth and claws adorned his chest.

Oksana said nothing. In her mind, it was not counsel but companionship that Dawntreader craved, and the task had fallen to her; none of his own tribemates seemed able to face him in his melancholy.

"Had he died among the Get," Sergiy said, "they would have hailed him as a hero born. But that he perished among strangers before his fifth year of changing…there will be strife."

Staring into the clear, placid spring, Oksana could not argue. The Get, while ferocious in battle, were not easily reasoned with. Wyrmbane's death would undoubtedly be a source of, as Sergiy put it, strife.

"Do you believe the young Fang's account?" he asked her. "Do your stormcrows tell you anything that would place his word in doubt?"

Oksana managed not to stiffen. This was the first time Dawntreader had ever mentioned the spirit birds. She reminded herself again that there was no inherent impropriety in her sending and receiving messengers from without the sept. But was Sergiy's question only what it appeared, or did it signal something more: distrust, suspicion? "Do I doubt his word that Lord Arkady commanded a minion of the Wyrm, that it bowed down before him? Why would Svorenko lie about his own cousin, a noble lord of the Fangs?"

"Not a lie, then. Could he be mistaken?" Sergiy wondered aloud.

"The possibility exists."

"He spoke of a tribemate of yours," Dawntreader continued.

"Yes," Oksana said, knowing that probing questions could lead her into dangerous territory, thanks to damnable Bily. "He did. This Yaroslav Ivanovych Neyizhsalo. I have heard the name but never met him." All true, she reminded herself. All true. "From what Svorenko says, Neyizhsalo planned to alert the sept of this Wyrm pit, had not Arkady intervened."

"That is what Svorenko says."

"If only Arkady had brought the fosterlings back here…" Oksana suggested reasonably.

"If only…" Sergiy echoed, shaking his head morosely. "But now there will be strife." He took a deep breath. "Tonight I will take ten strong warriors. We will deal with this Wyrm pit, and perhaps find sign of Lord Arkady, as well."

Perhaps they would, at that, Oksana thought.

"After the next full moon, once the rites have been performed, you will take Wyrmbane's body back to his sept. And bring back our fosterling, I suppose. I don't imagine the Get will look favorably on continuing the exchange."

"I feel…responsible, Sergiy," Oksana said, allowing genuine emotion to soothe the edges of the half-truths she spoke. "The fosterlings between septs was my suggestion…."

"Now, now, my Oksana Yahnivna." Dawntreader placed his great hand against her cheek with supreme gentleness. "How could you have known?" His words and the depths of his distress tugged at Oksana, at what she knew to be true, but she

held firm. "Ah, perhaps some good will still come of this trag-
edy," he sighed, sounding far from convinced.

"We must be certain that it does," Oksana said, placing her
hand over his.

Chapter 18

There was no two ways about it: The wretched tune was stuck in Korda Laszlo's head. Three times today he thought he'd banished it, and thrice he'd again caught himself humming. The verses themselves were innocuous enough, if a bit forced in their rhyme scheme, but the refrain—the refrain was catchy, in a infuriatingly inane way: *Wherever goes Konietzko/there it is that I go....* Blah, blah, blah, blah, blah.... *Lord of the Night Sky/ stand by his side till doom is nigh.*

The margrave would be flayed alive before admitting it, but Laszlo had heard *him* humming the song last night. Perhaps Gryffyth SeaFoam had earned his keep. Time would tell.

For the time being, Laszlo hoped that official matters would occupy his full attention and keep the tune at bay. He had kept the woman waiting for over an hour, alone in the audience chamber. He'd looked in on her, surreptitiously, in that time. There had, of course, been legitimate needs he'd been attending to, but minor duties, one and all; he could easily have set them aside and seen her more promptly. But there was merit in establishing whose priorities took precedence, whose time was more valuable. Having accomplished that, Laszlo looked forward to speaking with her.

She was as lithe and lovely as he remembered; her dark hair would not be touched by gray for many years still. Laszlo offered her his hands as she rose from her seat by the brazier. "It is well that you arrived safely, Oksana Yahnivna Maslov," he greeted her formally in Ukrainian.

She took his hands and bowed her head. "Your hospitality does me great honor, Korda Laszlo."

"It is you who deserves honor," he said, indicating with a

gesture that she should resume her seat. "I have heard, over the past fortnight, many hushed tidings from your sept, and from others in Russia: that Lord Arkady is missing, and whispers of Wyrm-taint again follow his name; that his kin, his own cousin, stands as his accuser; that reluctant Queen Tamara of the Fangs cannot this time turn a deaf ear."

"I hear much the same," Oksana said. "It is fortunate that your stormcrow brought me tidings of Child Marrow and his underling. Bily did seek me out, as you'd suspected he might."

Laszlo accepted her praise graciously; there was only danger in gloating. He didn't dare mention the informant within Eduard Sun-Curser's dank halls at the Sept of the Brooding Sky; far better for each link of the shadow moot to know as little as possible about the others. "Again, you deserve the honor, Oksana Yahnivna. I but alerted you. It was you who turned Bily and the Sun-Curser's scheme to our advantage. I can understand their desire to see Arkady dead, but he is so much more useful *alive*: rumors of Wyrm-taint among the Fangs; Queen Tamara facing criticism whether she acts or doesn't act against him; and there is the reaction of House Gleaming Eye to consider in all of this, as well."

"It was more than we could have hoped," Oksana added demurely, "that, after receiving my warning, Arkady would exhibit what might very well be Wyrm taint in combating that beast."

"What became of the Thunderwyrm?" Laszlo asked. "I hear that Dawntreader was not pleased that it was relatively close to the caern."

"Displeased by that, and by the fact that the fomori at the village seemed the type to nest with a Bane more than a Thunderwyrm. Perhaps they called forth the Thunderwyrm as part of their trap, but no one knows. And Dawntreader was displeased by the death of a fosterling in his care, and of a sweet, young girl...." Oksana spoke softly as she enumerated the sept leader's grievances.

Laszlo watched her intently. Perhaps she was growing too close to Dawntreader, he thought. That, after all, was why he had summoned her here: to ascertain her fitness to continue as agent within the Sept of the Dawn. Messengers could relay details of events easily enough, but disposition and state of mind—those were trickier. Dawntreader had a way of gaining a person's trust and loyalty, even against his or her better judgment. Perhaps Oksana should be removed and replaced by someone else. As she informed Laszlo of the goings-on east of the mountains, he could see that, at the very least, Oksana was in awe of Dawntreader. "I see. And what of the Wyrm pit?" Laszlo asked, impatient; he was concerned with the implications, not the details, of her sentimentality.

"He took warriors the next night," Oksana said, "but found sign of neither Thunderwyrm, nor Bane, nor Arkady."

"Dawntreader cleansed the land, then?"

"He did," Oksana said. "I was not present, but I have heard the stories. The Galliards tell that he sat for three days and three nights at that place, fasting and meditating and communing with the spirits. They say that at the next dawn, he stood and opened a vein in his wrist. His blood ran into the pit, and almost at once water bubbled up from the earth. They say it was Gaia weeping for his pain. They say that Dawntreader does not discover caerns but creates them, as he did at the Sept of the Dawn."

"An amazing gift," Laszlo said admiringly, "and one that is very valuable to us." He paused to reconsider his thought that Oksana should be removed from the Sept of the Dawn. Sergiy Dawntreader would be a force in the revitalization of Eastern Europe, in the reclamation of the region for the Garou. And favorably inclined toward the Shadow Lords, he might become a useful ally in the quest for a unified Garou Nation. Perhaps, despite her potential burgeoning attachment, *because* of that attachment, Oksana might be the perfect agent to leave in place, rather than replace. Situations might simply arise when the full details of circumstances would need to be kept from her— to ensure that she acted in the best interest of the tribe. Her attachments would make her predictable, and her predictability would allow Laszlo to control her.

"Ah," he said, realizing that she was watching him and thinking perhaps that he still contemplated the majesty of

Dawntreader's gift of cleansing. "What awaits you back east of the mountains?" he asked.

"A dead fosterling," Oksana said morosely, "and a trek to the Sept of the Anvil-Klaiven."

Laszlo tsked. "The Get will not take kindly to their loss."

Oksana shook her head. "I would expect not."

"Well, be sure to guard your health—and your back. There is no telling what that tribe of brutes and killers might attempt. They are not so refined as you and me."

Laszlo stood and prepared to leave her then, but he noticed how she remained seated, expectantly. "Was there something else?" he asked.

Oksana seemed at a loss for words momentarily. She glanced around the audience chamber. "The margrave...?"

"Occupied, at present," Laszlo said. "Far too busy to grant an audience just now. Additionally, as so few people know of your connection to this sept, it would not do for you to be seen with him personally. Your coming here is as much a risk as we dare."

"I see."

"Yes...well, then. Please be sure to use the passage by which you entered. It is much less...*public* than others."

"As you wish." Oksana stood and bowed formally. "May Sister Luna watch over you, and Mother Gaia embrace you, Korda Laszlo."

"And may their blessings flow over you like water," he replied. With a curt bow of his own, Laszlo turned his back on her and moved on to other pressing matters. He didn't realize until much later that he was humming to himself.

Chapter 19

Oksana did not right away leave the fortress beneath the mountain. Many years had passed since she had last visited the Sept of the Night Sky. She had been a girl then, and Boris Thunderstrike had been leader. Tonight, she had studied raptly the tapestry in the audience chamber while Korda Laszlo had kept her waiting. Thunderstrike, one of the greatest personages of the Shadow Lords, had served as beta to a Silver Fang, Heart-of-Fury, before wresting control of the caern for the Lords and coming into his own as alpha. Surely Laszlo, even in his condescension, knew the story.

Echoes of the past joined those of Oksana's footsteps as she made her way unerringly toward the private chambers. Her earliest memories were of these stone corridors, before she and her mother had been whisked away to be part of the human world—the whispered world of Kinfolk. Often there had been voices at night, unseen visitors speaking to her mother—and the birds. More than once Oksana had awoken terrified in the night to the clatter of wings buffeting the windows of her home, talons scratching at the sills. Always her mother had spoken harshly, chastising a paranoid girl and her tears, and sent her back to bed.

But in the morning, Oksana would find the feathers. Outside, beneath the windows. Raven feathers, black as the darkest night. She had saved them and woven them together. Only years later had she come to realize the power of her childhood fetish.

Tracing her route with care, Oksana paused before a stout wooden door. The directions she followed were precise. Laszlo's stormcrow was not the only spirit bird to visit her. She paused and studied the grains of the door. Strange, she thought, to be called back after so many years of exile. Even after her first change, she had been sent to another sept to learn the ways of the Garou, by then merely vague memories from her earliest years. Soon, the ravens and stormcrows had come for her and not her mother, who had seemed abandoned, forgotten, once her little girl was gone. The woman had been winnowed, in spirit if not in body, until she was but an empty husk of a person. Probably she had died since then. Oksana did not know. Her mother was not full Garou.

Oksana knocked quietly but firmly on the door. Footsteps from the other side, and then it opened. Margrave Konietzko ushered her within.

She had met him twice before, clandestinely both times. He was as tall and finely muscled as she remembered. Oksana hoped some day to see him in battle, powerful arms wielding his massive sword like the wrath of Grandfather Thunder, knotted legs braced against Mother Gaia as he resisted legions of Wyrm-spawn. The margrave's silvery mane and beard were neat but not preened.

The door closed, he studied her. There was nothing soft about the steely gaze of his black eyes, nothing sentimental. "Oksana," he said, and only in his voice was there the slightest hint of the effort required for him to speak her name. "I am pleased..." he paused, began again, "The reports I receive of your activities are encouraging."

Oksana bowed. She tried to keep her eyes lowered in deference, but her glance was irresistibly drawn upward, toward his solid chest, the sweep of his glistening hair, his strong features and uncompromising eyes. She looked away instead, at the sparse furnishings of the room: a few wooden chairs, a small table, a hard cot with a single fur for bedding. This was not a room for family; it was not living quarters but a way station, brief respite from war and struggle and swirling violence.

"Your and Laszlo's suspicions of the Sun-Curser proved well-founded," she said at last. The statement felt out of place, but really it was *she* who was out of place, and neither she nor the margrave seemed able to speak beyond matters of the tribe.

Konietzko grew more at ease. "Yes. He will have to be dealt with. His bald opportunism and the stench of Wyrm-taint that rises from his lair undermine all that we build. He is little better than the Fangs."

"It seems the Fangs carry their own taint," Oksana said. That was as much as she would say; she knew the ways of these political circles: The margrave might have received "encouraging" word of her activities, but he wouldn't know, *or want to know*, the details of how she'd turned aside Bily's scheme with one of her own, how she was responsible for the death of a brave fosterling. The shadow moot was the province of Laszlo; the margrave would see only the results: that Arkady was tainted, that Sun-Curser was a threat because, unlike Laszlo and Oksana, he plied his treachery too boldly. Garou of other tribes mistrusted or reviled the alpha of the Brooding Sky Sept, while increasingly they respected and honored Konietzko. The margrave, foremost of the Lords, stood upon the backs of those like Oksana and Laszlo; he benefited from their labor but did not dirty his own hands—as it should be.

"I did not ask you here to speak of Lord Arkady," Konietzko said. His brow furrowed as he stepped toward Oksana and grasped her shoulders in his strong hands. "The end of our struggle is drawing near," he said, holding her gaze with his own. "Nearer than many realize or are willing to admit. There will be many sacrifices that we must make...." He paused. His gaze bore into Oksana; she came close to drawing away, but the margrave held her firmly. "Painful sacrifices, but necessary." Again he paused, watching her, studying her. Searching for some sign of recognition.

Oksana wanted to tell him that she understood. Had she not already sacrificed her first home, her mother, her place among the Lords, and perhaps her honor? But as fiercely as his fingers held her shoulders, his gaze held her silent, as well.

"There will come a time soon," Konietzko said, "when we will meet publicly, among other Garou. Choices will be made... and I wanted to see you, alone, once, before then. My daughter." He took her in his arms and crushed her against him.

Belatedly, Oksana returned his embrace. They were

awkward, both of them, unused to intimacy of spirit. And then it was over. Konietzko held her at arm's length again. He managed a sort of grim smile; he clapped her on the shoulder, as he might a warrior. She nodded curtly, and then Oksana left him.

Chapter 20

When another knock sounded at Konietzko's door, he was seated at the table, busying himself with his maps. "Enter." Korda Laszlo slipped into the small, spartanly furnished room. Konietzko did not look up from the table. "Yes?"

Laszlo bowed. "My lord Margrave, Swift-as-the-River has departed the caern." Laszlo waited, but Konietzko did not respond. "I thought you would want to know." The margrave nodded almost imperceptibly. "Helena Slow-to-Anger will be leaving soon, as well," Laszlo added.

"Anything else?" Konietzko asked gruffly.

"Nothing of consequence, my lord Margrave."

"You may go, then."

Laszlo started to back from the room.

"Laszlo," Konietzko said, still not looking up from his maps: one detailing every Leech sighting within one hundred kilometers of the caern over the past five years; the other a depiction of the Tisza River basin.

Laszlo stopped. "Yes, my lord?"

"You met tonight with the woman from Dawntreader's sept?"

"Yes, my lord."

"And your conclusion?"

"I believe she is capable of retaining Dawntreader's trust," Laszlo said.

"And serving us?"

"In one capacity or another, knowingly or unknowingly—yes."

"I see."

"Dawntreader has a way of turning those around him toward his own agenda," Laszlo said. "But that, too, can work in our favor."

"And she is gone now," Konietzko said, "the woman."

"Oksana Yahnivna Maslov. Yes, she is gone." Laszlo chuckled. "She seemed interested in meeting you—but of course there was no need."

"As you say," Konietzko said. "That will be all."

Laszlo began to raise another point but then wisely reconsidered, instead respecting the margrave's curt dismissal. When the door closed and Konietzko was again alone, he returned his attention to the maps from which he had not looked away. His thoughts, however, remained with Oksana.

He had noticed that she wore the belt he had given her years ago, carved from the tendons of his own thigh. He'd meant the gift to bind her to him, though time and great distance intervene between them, yet now he pondered the possibility that he had bound himself just as firmly to her, his first Garou child. The attachment was one he likely could not afford if he was to fulfill his destiny and unite the Garou nation behind him.

The maps. He reminded himself to study the maps. But his thoughts again wandered: this time not east with Oksana, but to the west and the north, where she would soon journey. All eyes, before long, would turn toward the Sept of the Anvil-Klaiven. Of that, Margrave Yuri Konietzko would make certain.

For Jason,
Who has waited overlong for his own song.

"Bitter the wind tonight
combing the sea's hair white:
from the North, no need to fear
the proud sea-coursing warrior."

—Ninth-century Irish monastic verse

Chapter 1

Karin Jarlsdottir barely managed to duck beneath the rack of antlers leveled at her head. The body of the stag pushed past her, nearly knocking her from her feet. The great beast's head dipped to clear the doorway as its momentum carried it right into the longhouse. There was a sudden riotous commotion of cooks, pigs and chickens inside.

Shaking her head in disbelief, Karin followed. From the open door, she surveyed the uproar. "Eighteen points," she said. "I swear he's got a full eighteen points if he has a single branching. Well done, Thijs! He is, by far, the proudest catch we've had today."

The antlers turned toward her again and bowed as if to receive her praise. Beneath the lolling head of the deer, she could see the fierce lupine grin of the hunter. Thijs was every inch as impressive a specimen as his prize. When his back wasn't bent beneath the weight of a stag, he stood well over nine feet in height.

"Well, if you're too stubborn to let anyone help you haul him back, you'll at least let me help you hang him," Karin said. She took a rope from a pile near the door and, uncoiling it, tossed one end up and over the rafters. "How far did you carry that monster anyway? Hold still now, so I can tie him off."

"Six miles, give or take," Thijs grunted and then let out a long, contented sigh as the rope lifted the weight from his back. He straightened and stretched luxuriously, muscles rippling.

Six miles with a three-hundred-pound deer on his back? Karin's shoulders ached at the mere thought of it. If she'd just gone through an ordeal like that, it would take a lot more than a good stretch to put her right again. Of course, she had absolutely no intention of confiding that fact to Thijs.

"And it wasn't stubborn," he protested. "The day I start letting some cubs tote my kills back to the caern! Well, that's the
day they start offering to cut my meat for me."

Karin hauled the massive carcass up with an ease that belied
her slight physique. Her body was taut and athletic, infused
with a restless energy, sensual in the same way the spring of
a great cat is sensual. She was as graceful as the well-placed
fall of a hammer. Power coupled with precision and purpose.
Karin was only in her mid-twenties, but the mantle of command rested comfortably on her shoulders. She was as at ease
dispensing praise or interpreting the law as in giving orders.

Her appearance was curious meeting of the trappings of
two very different millennia. Karin wore the traditional warrior-braid—a badge of honor straight out of the ninth century—
that reached halfway down her back. At her breast hung the
Mjollnir—the hammer-cross pendant of Thor—upon a leather
thong. Her leather jacket, however, was of the most contempo-
rary cut and straight from the shops of Firenze. It covered a mail
shirt of jeweler-fine rings crafted from a lightweight modern
alloy. The tails of the shirt hung down over a pair of American
jeans, ripped and grass-stained about the knees. The ensemble
was rounded out by a pair of mythical Seven-League Boots.

Karin deftly lashed off the free end of the rope, neither
unaware of nor displeased with the eyes that fawningly followed her every movement. The stag hung head-down, its
majestic rack of antlers nearly scraping the floor. Reaching out,
she carved Thijs's rune into the fur of the stag's brow with one
claw.

Thijs was beaming. "Beautiful," he murmured. Realizing
he had spoken aloud, he coughed to cover his embarrassment.
"Er, he is a beauty, is he not?" Thijs rocked back on his heels to
admire his kill. "And led me on quite a chase, I'll tell you. Why
it was barely midday when I first caught his scent..."

Sören, who had come up behind him carrying a long drip-
pings pan, interrupted Thijs with a laugh and a hearty slap on
the back. "If this beast is going to grace the head table, you'll
need a better tale than that. To listen to you tell it, a body would

think you've never so much as brought down a stringy winter hare before! It's lucky for you that you've still some time to work out the details before the feast. You don't bring down a fine specimen like this without having chased it for at least three days and three nights," he scolded.

"But the hunters were only sent out this morning. And everyone knows it," Thijs protested.

Shaking his head, the Master Hospitaler crossed to the stag and slid his pan beneath it. "You are a great moose. Now listen to your elders. What everyone knows," he said, "is that you don't bring down a stag like this without a story. Trust me, three days, three nights. And you might want to throw in something about having seen it in a vision first. Nothing too showy, mind you. Maybe you saw it standing silhouetted on a hilltop at the last full moon. And you knew it was the same stag because... because..."

He raised his head, examining the majestic beast in minute detail, searching for some distinguishing feature—the patch of silver at its breast, the crescent-moon scar upon its shoulder, the...

"The eighteen points," Karin whispered.

"The eighteen points!" the Hospitaler proclaimed triumphantly. "Clear as moonrise, you can count them yourself. No sir, there's no doubting a story like that."

Thijs looked skeptical. "You really think...?"

"Only when I absolutely have to," the Hospitaler interrupted in a conspiratorial whisper. "That's sound advice. It's served me well over the years and you're welcome to it." Before Thijs could object further, the Hospitaler tore a haunch of roast pork from the nearest spit and pressed it into the hunter's hand. He herded the younger Garou toward the door.

"Now if you will kindly quit stomping around my kitchens with those great clumsy paws of yours—frankly you're making the cooks nervous—we can all get back to work." He shooed Thijs out the door and the latter loped off toward the nearest knot of hunters. Sören noted that they were doing a poor job of concealing their craning interest in the huge stag that had just vanished within the House of the Spearsreach. He turned back toward the Jarlsdottir. "You don't think you could convince them to leave these things hanging outside somewhere?"

Karin smiled. "Wouldn't dream of it."

"It would be nice if the cooks could get a bit of work done in here without continually cracking their heads on some fool hunting trophy. If you ask me," he grumbled, peering at her from the corner of his eye, "I'd say you're more than slightly pleased at the thought of these proud young alphas parading up here to lay their kills at your feet."

With satisfaction, he saw her stiffen. He turned toward her, smiling his most disarming smile.

She realized immediately that he meant to offer neither offense nor formal challenge. He was only playing the flea—trying to find a sensitive spot in which to insinuate his barb. She visibly calmed. The challenges of late had been coming fast and furious and she was admittedly a bit on edge.

"I cannot bring myself to believe that your wits have grown as soft as your teeth, old skald," she said. "Surely you have not forgotten the little you once knew of love-play. The Jarl is never without suitors. These nights, there are more contests to see who would be first among them than challenges to my right to lead our people."

"You had me right up until the last," he said. "More suitors than challengers? You've been fighting since you first returned here to bury your father. And if any suitor had won through to your bower of late," he added slyly, "he would certainly not have been able to keep such a secret from me. You forget, perhaps, that I am the ears as well as the tongue of this sept."

"Ears can be boxed," she replied. "And some tongues wag to their owner's misfortune."

Ignoring the threat, he walked straight over to her and—before she could stop him or even object—placed a hand on her belly. He felt only taut muscle. "Prove me wrong," he said. "Nothing would please me more. The day that I feel the stirring of cubs here, you will have heard the end of a foolish old man's prattle."

"I will hold you to that," she replied indignantly. "And the day you next lay your hand upon me uninvited, I'll have it nailed to my doorpost."

He smiled broadly. "Uninvited, you say? That is promising. It clearly implies the possibility of other occasions on which it would be invited."

"You flatter yourself, old man. And you know very well that the Jarl's task is to lead the people in battle, to safeguard the sept, to sit in judgment. It is not to whelp cubs."

"Is it not the Jarl's duty to see to the life of the tribe?" he countered. "And to do so to the very limit of his strength and with every weapon at his disposal? If the Jarl is a hunter, he feeds his people. If he is an advocate of the law," he gazed at her pointedly, "he dispenses wisdom. And if the Jarl is the alpha female..."

"She should bear the tribe strong cubs. Yes, I've heard the argument before. This probably comes as no surprise to you, as you put it forward weekly. But, as you are also quick to point out, it is a constant battle to get them to submit to being led by a woman as things stand now. Can you imagine what it would be like if I had a bellyful of cubs? The challenges would be ceaseless. And if you think for one moment that I would put my unborn children in the middle of an Ascendancy Challenge..."

"They wouldn't dare!" he cried. "There is no honor in striking a woman, and only blackest infamy in raising a hand to a mother with-child. Why, I could make a second reputation solely on the rhymed Censure I might compose over such a coward who would presume to challenge a Jarl with-cub!"

"Ah, now we get to the root of your proddings. You are hearing the stealthy tread of Death-Comes-After. But you will not win your reputation or ride into Valhalla upon my skirts. Your time would be better spent composing verses to our young warriors."

"And what if I do hear the footsteps? What is that to you? Wodin save us from strong-headed women. I am only looking out for you, child, and for the future of your father's line. I fear for you, for what might happen to you once I am gone. At least while I live, I know I can lend my tongue—my last remaining weapon, but a sharp one!—to defending your right and honoring the memory of your father."

"Sören, listen to me. You were always my father's trusted

friend and most generous supporter. But you cannot give him grandchildren! You would not find the pangs to your liking and you would look quite the fool panting and squatting over—"

"There are some mysteries," he interrupted quickly, "that are better kept from mere men such as myself. I yield."

But he could not resist a parting shot as he turned away toward the door. "Although to my mind, the fastest way to stop these incessant challenges would be to announce that you were with cub."

She threw up her hands in exasperation. "You are a blackguard, Sören Hospitaler. You fight like a crow—yielding, and then continuing to peck away despite your pledge. And just what exactly do you think that would accomplish, my announcing that I was with cub? It would confuse them, that's certain. There's not much about cub-rearing that doesn't throw the lot of you into a disorderly retreat. But they'd regroup eventually. And then they would decide that the indignity of submitting to a whelping Jarl was simply too great to bear. They would proclaim a new sept leader on the spot."

He waved aside her objections. "And then, once you'd weaned the cubs, you would thrash the upstart the entire length of the Hammerfell, reclaim your rightful place and everyone would be hap—"

Sören broke off midsentence, staring out the doorway and toward the distant frostlit treeline. His visage darkened.

"What's wrong now, old skald?" Karin said. "Surely you haven't spotted another female without pups scurrying about her feet. As many times as we've supped together, I've never known you to be able to hold down your words any better than your drink."

Sören did not appear to hear her. "It seems we may have been overhasty in awarding laurels," he said in an ominous tone. "The Warder comes and bringing a prize the equal of any ten of Thijs's eighteen-pointers."

Something in his dark mood was contagious. Karin found her fists clenched white-knuckled upon the high back of the Jarl's Siege—the massive oaken chair at the table's head. Cursing herself for letting the storyteller get the better of her again, she forced her hands to relax. Still, all the bustle of the kitchens seemed to have ground to a standstill. The entire hall tensed, as if bracing for a hammer blow.

The Warder rolled through the doorway like a gathering storm. His brow was as low and dark as a thunderhead. Without a word of greeting, he made straight for the high table. At his passing, chickens scrambled behind table legs, children retreated behind the skirts of the cooks, and the cooks, in turn, withdrew back into the shelter of the pillars.

Draped across the Warder's arms was the body of a young man.

Sören had to strike into a loping run to keep pace with the Warder's long, determined strides. The Hospitaler was muttering incoherently. "Well, I'd not believe it.... I had said I wouldn't, all along. Not until I had seen it with my own eyes. Until I had put my hand into his wounds. And here he is, our wayward cub, come home to us at last. And us the sadder on the night of his homecoming than on that of his leave-taking. Oh, this is a dark day for our people. No question."

The Warder pointedly ignored him. He strode right up to the high table. With the back of one arm, he swept the board clear, sending the carefully prepared delicacies clattering to the floor in a rain of broken dishes and crockery.

With a thud he dropped the body upon the table before her.

"Here is my son, *Jarlsdottir*," he hurled the title like an invective. "Look upon him! You were of an age and you knew him of old. You were there when his teeth found the throat of the Icewyrm. You were there at the feasting that followed when he put aside his father's name. It was you who laid the mantle of his warrior-name upon him with your own hands. *Wyrmsbane*, you named him. And I was proud, Jarlsdottir. Swelled with father-pride. Do you remember, this, my son?" His stare was all ice and daggers, but there were tears at the corners of the old warrior's eyes. He made no effort to wipe them away or conceal them.

Karin met his gaze, unflinching. She was silent a long while. Her voice, when she mastered it at last, had a faraway note to it, as if reciting some ancient scripture. She laid her right hand upon the dead man's chest, asserting her claim, her right to grieve over him.

"Here is my shield-brother, Warder. Look upon him. When the Icewyrm ravaged the northern marches, he was the first into the fray. When my spear broke against the monster's scales, he handed me his own. When no blow availed against its armor, it was Arne who found the warm rush of its throat. We mourn for our fallen brother."

"Mourning is not enough, Jarlsdottir," the Warder barked. "What is your morning to me? Such coin I already have in abundance. Do I not have my own pack, my own women? I do not sell my son's life so cheaply."

"He will have a hero's burial. He has earned it three times over. Arne was a tireless warrior, not only in the crusade against the Wyrm, but also in peacetime—in his battles to heal the Rift. The people grieve with you, Brand Garmson. He will be sorely missed."

"It's not his burial rites that I require of you, Jarlsdottir. In my pack there are many strong backs to turn the earth. We can return our own to Gaia's bosom. What I want is justice. Blood calls to blood. You are the law-speaker. I demand the *wergild*— the blood price. I will have vengeance upon those who killed my son."

"Brand, I understand your anger and your hurt. It is not yet three summers since we buried my father, you and I. And on that occasion, I was glad enough for your strength and your good counsel. Now let me repay some small measure of that debt in turn." She came forward and took him by one arm, but he refused to be turned or budged.

"Vengeance will not restore Arne to you," she said. She could see the raw emotion shuddering through him, the howl of grief fighting its way to the surface. His muscles bunched and surged under the force of it, warping his body into the lupine form that might give it proper voice. The effort of fighting that change was plain on his features. She held him firm and continued to pour bolstering words, like strong drink, into him. "And calling for blood will likely undo all that Arne strove to accomplish these last years. He went into this arrangement with his eyes open and his claws sheathed. It was nobly done, and there wasn't another one among us who might have shouldered the burden half as well. Not you, certainly not I. And if it came to a sad end, that does not diminish the glory of it. He has brought great honor to your house, and to our sept, and, I believe, to our entire tribe. Be content. Let us honor the dead, not seek to swell their ranks further."

But the wolf in him already had the upper hand and he did not or could not heed her words. "The *wergild*," he growled, low and threatening. "It is my right. You will not deny me." Already his vocal chords were having difficulties bending themselves around the niceties of human speech. He sank to his haunches before her, curling in upon himself.

She sat back on her heels, keeping her gaze level with his, holding his eyes. His face stretched into a long, grizzled gray muzzle. The great clenched jaws were broad enough that, should they turn on her, they might snap closed over her entire head.

"Brand, our cousins at the Sept of the Dawn, they did not kill your son. They are not responsible for his death. You were in this hall when their runner arrived. He said Arne fell in honorable battle against the forces of the Wyrm. We cannot hold his hosts to blame."

"I will know more," the Warder snapped. "Oh, yes. I will question their emissary. I will have from her her secrets. I will hold her to account."

"What are you talking about?" Karin replied. "*Her* who?" Then realization dawned. "Who has brought the body back to us for burial? Why has this ambassador not presented herself before me and given the first-hand account we have been so anxiously awaiting these past nights?"

"Our patrols intercepted her as she approached the bawn. A Shadow Lord," his muzzle twisted the name into a hiss of spite. "Sent here armed with lies and platitudes. But I'll have her story from her, or her pelt!"

A look of horror spread over Karin's face. She barked orders to the Hospitaler, but her eyes never left those of the Warder. "Sören. Get out there to Brand's pack, now. Take any of the hunters that are still hanging about outside with you and go quickly. The ambassador from the Sept of the Dawn is to be brought to me here, immediately. And unharmed. By my personal order in the presence of yourself and the Warder. Damn it, Brand, if you or any of your boys have harmed that messenger..."

Brand's only answer was a inhuman growl. He wore his hulking dire-wolf form, his pelt the menacing gray of shadows upon the ice floe. Sören backed away carefully toward the doorway, wary of making any sudden moves.

"I would not, old man," Brand threatened. "Another step and you will feel my fangs."

"You will not countermand my orders, Warder." Karin rose to her full height. "Nor waylay those upon the Jarl's business." She was shifting as she spoke.

In her warrior-form, Karin towered well over eight feet in height. Her wiry muscles swelled to tree-rending proportions. Lustrous silver-tinted fur covered her from tip to toe, the long warrior-braid trailing out behind her.

"No, Jarlsdottir," came the answering growl. "You mistake me. I will drag my prey before you myself. It is my right. My duty." The hulking wolf turned disdainfully and stalked toward the door.

Her voice cut sharply across the longhouse. "Your place is here, Warder. With Arne. *Do you remember, this, your son?*"

Her rebuke brought him up short as if pierced by silver. He half-turned and there was again the engulfing sadness in his eyes. "You look to the dead, Jarlsdottir. I will seek their vengeance among the living."

He stalked from the House of the Spearsreach and out into the first light of the rising moon. And then he could contain it no longer. Brand Garmson, Warder of the Sept of the Anvil-Klaiven, threw back his head and howled. All across the bawn, troubled faces looked up from their work and knew that the Stalker-at-the-End-of-Days was once again come among them.

Chapter 2

There was a dark aspect to the party that crossed the Aeld Baile toward the House of the Spearsreach. At its head stalked Brand Garmson. He approached the hall of the Jarlsdottir with drawn steel and silver. At his passing, Kinfolk and Garou alike shrank back from him, from the grief that consumed him. It was a fearsome passion, as terrible to behold as the *berserke* warrior-rage.

The honor guard that followed hot upon the Warder's heels was no funeral escort. The Warder's party was composed of four other hulking Arhoun warriors. Their massive frames all but eclipsed the small dark woman in their midst. Oksana Yahnivna walked erect, head thrown back, proud and defiant. A regal ermine-trimmed cloak streamed from her shoulders. Many who craned to catch a glimpse of the stranger were struck by her noble bearing. They wondered at her presence here, at what it portended, at what crime she had committed.

Each of her four escorts wore the Executioner's Form—the powerful human body crowned by a gnashing lupine head. It was one of the legendary Abhorrent Visages—which, according to the Fenrir lore keepers, traced their lineage all the way back to the Impergium. The Executioner's Form was an amazingly taxing transformation and the strain of maintaining it only added to the party's savage demeanor.

Karin Jarlsdottir intercepted them partway across the Aeld Baile. Catching sight of her, the Warder raised his hand for a halt. His bow was exaggerated, bordering on the mocking. When he had straightened, his voice boomed out. "As you command, Jarlsdottir, it is done. I have brought the spy from the Sept of the Dawn. She—"

Karin pitched her voice so that it might carry across the frozen yard to the figures that hung back in the shadows of the surrounding doorways. "Thank you, Warder, for seeing our guest here safely. You may disperse your escort and put up your arms."

"Perhaps the Jarlsdottir does not understand." Each word was an effort for him. "This is the traitorous..."

Ignoring him, Karin brushed past and took the small dark woman by the arm to draw her from the midst of the cordon of warriors. The gesture seemed to startle the newcomer even more than the Warder. For a moment it seemed Oksana might recoil from her, from the presumption, the familiarity of that contact. She immediately thought better of it. Slowly, deliberately, Oksana entwined her fingers in Karin's and squeezed. She allowed herself to be led from the circle.

"We will talk further inside," Karin said, patting Oksana's arm reassuringly. "Join us, Warder. What the ambassador has to say will surely be of interest to you."

She pointedly turned her back on him and led her guest toward the hall. Karin counted off the paces silently, expecting at any moment the bellowed challenge from the Warder. One pace, two, three...

She heard a sharp growl from behind. "Gaia preserve us from the conniving of her daughters! You four, return to the periphery. I want the patrols doubled. I will look after this prisoner myself." His angry footfalls pounded closer through the packed snow. Karin smiled.

They swept into the hall only to find themselves set upon by a horde of new assailants. Cooks pressed them sorely with steaming platters—each plate heaped high with roast pork and small, sour winter's apples. Children rushed their flank, leveling prodigious horns of sloshing ale. Oksana found herself all but buried beneath a cavalry charge of provisions.

Karin lost her grip on her guest somewhere in the fray. She could only watch as the tide of battle swept Oksana away toward the high table. Behind her, there was the sudden clang of a brass serving platter rebounding off a wall. It was followed shortly by the Warder's cursing as he cut a swath through the forces arrayed before him, scattering them, driving them from the field.

She moved to block his advance and planted one hand firmly in the center of his chest. He took two more steps forward, his momentum carrying her backwards, her feet sliding across the layer of reeds and straw covering the packed-earth floor. When the two at last came to rest, her voice was little more than a whisper. "You will not offer any further insult to our guest. You have done quite enough already. At this point, you are here only because I believe that this woman might well have something to tell us about the death of Arne Wyrmsbane. It is fitting that you should hear this news firsthand, but if you will not control yourself, I will not hesitate to turn you out. Do I make myself clear, Warder?"

He glared at her. "If she says one thing, Jarlsdottir—one!— against my son, I will gut her where she stands."

"She will not dishonor my shield-brother within my hall," Karin said. "Or she will have far more to answer to than your claws alone, old wolf. Now let us hear what she has to say."

He scowled back at her, and then stomped off toward his accustomed place at the high table. Karin shooed the last of the plate- and cup-bearers out from underfoot. She straightened to her full height and self-consciously pushed her hair back behind one ear. Smoothing at the wrinkles in her worn leather jacket didn't seem to help. It would not hang right, but looked as if she had slept in it. *I've done far worse than* sleep *in it*, she thought. *All things considered, it's holding up remarkably well.* She hoped the same thing might be said about her, but suspected that by this point she must have been looking a little frayed about the edges.

The sight of her guest did little to set Karin's mind at ease. The ambassador was proud, regal, beautiful. Karin could not quite keep her mind from certain unflattering comparisons. She was willing to bet that the petite and lithe newcomer had never once had to resign herself to being several inches taller than the boys her own age. Karin's physique had always been much more suited to the ballpitch than the ballroom.

She stood directly before her guest, towering over her. Her first rush of words sounded overloud at such close quarters.

"Here we have a custom, food before fine words. Know that you are welcome here, doubly so as you have brought one of our own home to us. I am Karin Jarlsdottir, Jarl of the Sept of the Anvil-Klaiven. This is my house, you need fear nothing here. There will be time for introductions and news of your journey after you have rested and eaten." Karin glared at the Warder, but he only grunted and set ravenously upon the food before him.

It was nearly an hour later when the last of them capitulated. Although they had given it a good effort, there was never really any hope of emptying a plate or a drinking horn as quickly as it was refilled.

"I thank you for your hospitality, Karin Jarlsdottir. I am Oksana Yahnivna of the Sept of the Dawn." She turned a lofty look upon the Warder. "It has often been my pleasure to sup with the son; it is my honor to dine with the father. I am only sorry my visit could not have been in more pleasant circumstances."

"You do us honor, Oksana Yahnivna," Karin cut in quickly before the Warder could reply. "Although we grieve for our fallen brother, we could not have hoped for better circumstances to come together. You have brought our shield-brother home to us. For this, you are deserving of a place of honor here. You have already met the Warder, Brand Garmson. Brand is Arne's..."

"His father. Yes, he talked of you often. You can be very proud of him, Warder. Your son was a fearless warrior. I was at the Sept of the Dawn the day that he first came to us. I think I can say that we are all stronger for his coming, even if he was among us for only a short time. Know that Arne died a hero's death—fallen in honorable combat against a Knockerwyrm—a fierce beast that had bored its way into an abandoned tin mine near the sept. By his sacrifice, Arne saved many other lives. His deeds will not be forgotten."

Brand growled. "Arne had fought wyrms many times before. The Jarlsdottir will attest to that. And he'd taken down more than one in single combat. How is it that this one escaped the bite of his axe? Or do you admit that the reek of corruption is that much stronger around the Sept of the Dawn? That the Russian wyrmlings are far more hearty than their humble cousins among the Icewyrms of the Fjords?"

"I have no knowledge whatsoever of your Icewyrms, and thus would not like to venture a comparison." Oksana's tone was haughty and cool. Her implication was clearly that the Warder should follow her example and keep silent about things of which he had no knowledge. It was not lost on the Warder. He bristled.

"How dare you? Because of you and yours, my son is now dead. He was entrusted to your care. Instead of safeguarding him, you sent him out, alone, to fight your battles for you. That was cowardly done. And the shame of that misdeed will hound you. I cannot believe that I ever allowed the boy to go into solitary peril among you. If only he had had his packmates around him! No three wyrmlings can hope to stand before a pack of Fenrir."

"No one sent your son into battle alone, Warder," Oksana said. "He had other warriors at his side. Several of whom—"

"Children!" Garmson interrupted. "Cubs and innocents. Why I've yet to meet the Child of Gaia capable of even sharpening her own claws properly—without agonizing over the harm it might do to the tree!" He slammed one hand down onto the massive oaken tabletop. Vicious claws sank to the knuckle, the force of the blow sending the platters leaping into the air. Brand had to brace his other hand on the table in order to free the first. As he wrenched it loose, it left four deep gouges in its wake.

"I understand that you are distraught, Warder. But I have lived at the Sept of the Dawn for many years now, and I can assure you that the Warriors of Gaia are fearsome to behold when roused to anger. But Arne's companions were not of the Gaians. He was accompanied by a Shadow Lord and two Silver Fangs."

"More fosterlings," Brand scoffed. "Cubs, and runts at that. When the Fenrir send a representative to the tribes, we send the best among us. I understand that other tribes show no such scruples. Why, look at that blasphemous inbred excuse for a..."

Karin's voice cut him off sharply. "That is enough, Warder. You have gone well over the line. You have our apologies, Oksana Yahnivna." She glanced sharply at Brand, expecting his immediate apology as well.

"But do I speak truth? Answer me that and I will be silent! We both know what coin we have received from our 'brothers and sisters' at the Sept of the Dawn. Why it's as clear as the horns on—"

"Enough!" Karin shouted. She rose from her seat and towered over the Warder. "This guest has come to honor our dead. You owe her a personal debt of honor on top of the courtesy you owe to all visitors to this house. I will not have you..."

Oksana placed a hand on Karin's arm. "The Warder was momentarily mastered by his grief. We do not hold his hot words against him. If he will hear me out, I will tell of Arne's battle against the Knockerwyrm. If this is not a good time..."

Brand was fuming, but his voice was low and steady. "Make no mistake, shadowling. You will not leave this house without telling me what I have come here to know."

She chose to ignore the threat. "Excellent. Please be seated, and I will speak. Arne Wyrmsbane did not go into battle alone, but alongside one of the most legendary living warriors of the Garou nation. He fought alongside none other than Lord Arkady of House Crescent Moon—"

"Arkady?" Garmson was on his feet again. "Surely not the same Arkady? Even as isolated as we are here, we have heard the tale of the Silver Crown and the ascension of King Albrecht to the throne of the Silver Fangs. They say that Albrecht banished Arkady—and for wyrm-taint! This is the guardian you entrusted my son to? Never in my lifetime has anyone played me and my kin so falsely! You have heard her words, Jarlsdottir. Her own words! Does she deny it?"

"Surely, Oksana Yahnivna does not mean..." Karin began, but then broke off at seeing the confirmation in her guest's eyes.

"Does she deny it?!" Brand insisted.

"I deny nothing," Oksana said. "I am not on trial here. Lord Arkady was visiting the sept. Your son—of his own will—accompanied Arkady. Arne was no hairless cub, Warder. Even when he first came to us, he was already past his Naming, and free to choose for himself. Two other warriors rounded out his hunting party. The first was Victor Svorenko, the Silver Fang fosterling, a friend and boon companion to Arne. During your son's stay at the sept, the two were inseparable. The other was the Shadow Lord, Andrey Neyizhsalo. All four members of the party were formidable warriors. When the party decided to set out on the trail of the wyrmbeast, they did not consult with Sergiy Dawntreader. They left without either his foreknowledge or his sanction. If you know anything of the Dawntreader, you know he is ever first into the fray. It is not his habit to send his people into solitary peril. That said, the expedition was well and nobly done all the same. There is no honor in shirking an opportunity when it presents itself."

Oksana had learned the tale by heart from Victor Svorenko and related it in its entirety. She was determined to withhold nothing. She told of the battle with the three fomori at the house of the goatherd, and of the subsequent quest to discover the tin mine, the epicenter of the corruption. She told of Arne's heroic fall—rent asunder in the jaws of the Knockerwyrm. She reported Victor's unsettling account of Lord Arkady's quelling the beast—of his unnatural sway of the minions of the Wyrm. And finally, she told how Victor bore the body of his companion safely back to the Sept of the Dawn.

When she had finished, they sat in silence for a time. The fight seemed to have gone out of the Warder. The story of his son's death had closed a circle—in a way that not even the immediacy of the boy's broken body could accomplish. The tale told, something deep inside Brand Garmson sealed itself up. Something that would not likely see the light of moon again.

He did not want to think back upon the time they had spent together. There was pain there, and self-reproach, and slow roiling rage.

Somewhere inside him there was a memory of a younger Arne, a streak of silver skidding across the ice floe, a cub on his first hunt. Brand let the weight of ice close over the boy, swallow him up.

Somewhere, a spear dangled forgotten from Arne's paw as he stooped in horror over the body of his shield-brother. A boisterous struggle for supremacy among cubs, gone too far. Brand watched as the spilled blood rose like a flood tide until it drowned the two boys entirely.

Somewhere, Brand, already twenty lengths ahead of his pack, raced desperately across the bawn toward his son's howl of alarm. He arrived only to find the boy muzzle-deep in the shredded remains of the Bane that the skalds would later name Creeping-Death-in-the-Extremities. His first kill. Brand could remember having to carry his son the entire way back to the longhouse. The boy's feet were little more than blackened and frozen stumps.

Years later, sitting in the House of the Spearsreach, the Warder turned his back upon the crippled memory and left it to make its own way home.

When he returned to the present, there was steel in his gaze and an unnerving calm that presaged violent storms just over the horizon. The two women were conversing in hushed tones.

"You have our thanks, Oksana Yahnivna. You will stay and be our honored guest for Arne's funeral rites," Karin said.

"I thank you for your generous offer of hospitality, but I think my presence here will only serve to keep the wound fresh. It is better that I go as soon as my mission here is complete."

"You must do as you think best," Karin said. "You have carried out your task admirably. I know it was not an easy one and you will be glad to be back among your people again as soon as may be. When you return, will you deliver a gift to Sergiy Dawntreader for me? I would like for him to know that I hold no animosity toward him nor toward your people for what has happened."

"I would be honored," Oksana said. "You are a kind and generous leader, Karin Jarlsdottir. I will look forward to tales of great things from the Sept of the Anvil-Klaiven in the future. If I may speak frankly, I did not know what sort of reception lay in store for me here. I am glad that I found you at the end of the journey. I have only one further boon to ask of you and I will take my leave."

Oksana's eyes dropped as she allowed the pause to stretch. She more than half hoped that Karin would chime in with one of those sweeping offers of largess for which the Fenrir were renowned. In this, Oksana was disappointed. In Karin, the Fenrir's characteristic full-moon passions—the legendary indulgences in lavish gifts, loveplay and warrior-rage—were tempered with a balanced half-moon's prudence and wisdom.

"What is it that you would ask of us, Oksana Yahnivna?"

Oksana tried to sound casual, as if what she requested were really something quite trivial and innocuous. "I would see the fosterling, Cries Havoc. He will also have an interest in the news I bear and I would like to deliver it personally. There are certain…forms that should be observed in these situations. He must be made aware of them, lest he inadvertently cause your people further pain before our departure."

At this last pronouncement, the Warder stirred from his reverie. His voice was icy calm. "The boy knows already. He has known since word first reached us that Arne was…that our own fosterling would not be returning. And he knows what that means. He knew what he was getting into before he ever departed your sept. Please spare us this prattle about travel plans. You know as well as we do that it is out of the question. Cries Havoc is not going anywhere."

Chapter 3

Oksana turned upon him a look of surprise as if the very thought had never occurred to her. "What do you mean, Warder? Surely Cries Havoc is not a prisoner here? He is Garou, a guest among you and free to come and go as he chooses."

"He was a peace hostage," the Warder said. "His life was surety for my son's. Now it is forfeit. It is the *wergild*, the blood price. If we had been so careless as to allow Cries Havoc to come to harm while under our protection, we should not expect Arne's return. But you know all this. Why do you play the starry-eyed cub for us?"

Oksana, looking wounded, turned upon Karin. "Is this true? Surely you don't intend to... No, it is unspeakable! I will see Cries Havoc at once. If you have harmed him—"

"Please, calm yourself, Oksana Yahnivna. Cries Havoc is well and you will see him shortly. But the Warder is correct, he cannot return to the Sept of the Dawn with you."

The Margrave Yuri Konietzko crouched upon the exposed crag face. The hill bore his name. It was his silent place, his still-point. The eye of the hurricane of activity that revolved around the prominent Shadow Lord. He felt, rather than heard, the intrusion into his windswept sanctum—the flutter of black wings. The shrill cry of the stormcrow.

The bird alighted on a boulder nearby and cocked its head, regarding him curiously. Konietzko could see immediately that this was no ordinary crow. It reminded him of a child's chalk drawing—the creature's outline was too pronounced, each feather standing out in sharp relief. And there was a quality to the blackness of those feathers…like gazing into a hole between worlds.

When it opened its beak, a human voice issued forth. Yuri knew it well. It belonged to Oksana Yahnivna, and at the sound of his daughter's voice, the Margrave's initial irritation lost some of its stranglehold upon him. He forced the muscles in his neck and shoulders to unknot.

"Your pardon, Margrave. I have willfully intruded upon your meditations. I ask only that you hear my news before handing down just sentence upon the messenger." The crow again cocked its head sharply to one side, but this time the gesture seemed one of deference, of bowing before its master.

"Justice can be blind, but she is never deaf, Oksana Yahnivna. Speak and we will judge the severity of your trespass by your words."

"The situation is complex, but I will try to be brief. I am here at the Sept of the Anvil-Klaiven. Karin Jarlsdottir has called a Concolation. It is to occur at the next full moon. I think you should be here."

Yuri waved at her in annoyance. "The Jarlsdottir has no authority to call a Concolation. It takes no fewer than five elder Garou—representatives of five tribes—to call such a solemn gathering. And even if she were to somehow convince the requisite number of elders to go along with her, the moot would still not occur until another three moon-cycles had passed from the day of its calling. There is simply not time to get the word out to the tribes and for interested parties to journey to the site of the moot."

The crow struck nervously at the rock with its beak. It was not until she heard the incessant tapping that Oksana realized that not only her words, but also her growing agitation, were being communicated by the stormcrow. She forced herself to remain calm, and said simply, "Try telling her that."

With a snort of disgust, the Margrave turned his back upon the bird. But he considered its words. He calculated and then recalculated the current balance of power and prestige among the septs in northern Europe. "No," he said at last. "Jarlsdottir is too new. She just doesn't have the clout. She's a sept-leader and a law-speaker—and in either of those capacities she's going to command some respect. But to call the tribes? No one will come. No one will lend any credence to her presumption. Really, Oksana! I know the Get are a fiery people—and their cublike enthusiasms are their most endearing qualities—but some things just have to be done according to tradition."

"She's going to execute a Gaian fosterling."

The Margrave inhaled slowly, deliberately. He rubbed the bridge of his nose with both hands. "Garou do not kill Garou, Oksana. Jarlsdottir is a law-speaker. She is intimately familiar with our traditions. If this fosterling has committed some crime in her domain, she is going to sit in judgment over him. That is her right. It is also, I might add, strictly a local matter. And one in which she will not thank us for meddling."

"Cries Havoc—that's the Gaian fosterling—is not accused of any crime, Margrave. He is a victim of circumstance. You will recall some months back the briefing I sent you regarding Sergiy Dawntreader's latest initiative to bridge the rift between the tribes...."

The Margrave regarded the bird critically. It shuffled from foot to foot. "I remember it well," he said. "Although in that briefing the scheme was represented as being *your* initiative, if I recall correctly."

"The Margrave flatters his servant. I merely offered the Dawntreader our guidance in this matter."

"Go on," he said, his voice like a razor.

"As part of this initiative, we reached out to certain other septs with which we had diplomatic ties. We arranged an exchange of fosterlings, sending our best and brightest—the most promising of the newest generation of Garou, all veritable princes of the blood—into fosterage with the allied septs. They, in turn, each sent a fosterling to live among us, to learn our ways, to discover that the tribes can work together and strive together and prosper."

"Yes, yes. A noble sentiment. And this Cries Havoc was

sent among the Get, to the Sept of the Anvil-Klaiven? Why am I familiar with that name? Cries Havoc..."

"He is Dawntreader's sister-son," Oksana said, perhaps a bit too quickly. "The Get were never exactly what I would call happy with the arrangement. And they take everything so literally. I think they regarded the fosterlings more as peace hostages. They were pledging their alliance to our sept. If we should be attacked, the Get would come to our aid. Their fosterling was the surety for that pledge."

"Who is the Get fosterling?" the Margrave asked.

"He was called Arne Wyrmsbane, the son of Brand Garmson, Warder of the Sept of the Anvil-Klaiven."

"*Was?*" The Margrave shrewdly cut to the heart of the dilemma.

"Yes, Margrave. Arne fell in battle against a Knockerwyrm. The Warder, Garmson, is demanding the *wergild*—the blood price. His son was technically under our protection."

The Margrave shook his head. "A glaring oversight, Oksana. It is unworthy of you. How could you let the boy rush off to battle when you were pledged to keep him from harm? I cannot believe you would be so negligent. There is more you are not telling me. Why would you want that boy dead?"

The bird fluttered in alarm, nearly lifting itself from its precarious perch. "You mistake me, Margrave. I wished the boy no harm. But you can no more keep a Get from battle than you can keep a river from flowing downhill."

"It is often prudent to dam a river," the Margrave pointed out. "To keep it from destroying one's home during the flood season, for instance."

The crow bowed its head. "It is more foolish still to debate with the Margrave. I cede the point. You are also correct in thinking that there is more to this unpleasant business. When Arne Wyrmsbane fell, he was fighting alongside Lord Arkady of House..."

For a terrifying moment, Oksana had the impression that the Margrave would snatch up the bird in his claws. She jerked back, as if that action could avert the fatal blow.

"Arkady was there? Among you! And you did not see fit to

inform me?" He was clearly fighting for control. The tips of his claws could be seen jutting from his fingertips. His hand, half-extended, trembled with restraint.

The crow peeked out from beneath its wing. "You have yet to hear the worst, I am afraid, Margrave. Karin Jarlsdottir would put Arkady on trial for his part in the fosterling's death. For his crimes against the Garou. For consorting with the Wyrm."

"Even Albrecht," the Margrave intoned slowly, "was unable to make that charge stick. What makes you think the Jarlsdottir will succeed where her betters have failed? What makes you think Arkady will even take notice of these accusations?"

"There is new evidence to consider, firsthand evidence and from an unimpeachable source. Victor Svorenko, a Silver Fang, himself a prince of House Crescent Moon."

"Arkady's own flesh and blood. Very interesting. I would know more. We shall delay holding you to account for your glaring oversights and your trespasses until we see you in person. You will please inform the Jarlsdottir that we would be delighted to accept her generous invitation."

The crow bowed its head until it touched the rock on which it was perched and then leapt into the air, wings beating fiercely for altitude and freedom.

Chapter 4

Sören Hospitaler was a whirlwind loosed among the long-houses. He seemed to be everywhere at once. A steady stream of runners from the kitchens, the guesthall and the out-lying patrols kept him appraised of all the latest catastrophes.

Guests were pouring into the sept at this point. He had already met (and broken up scuffles between) visitors from as far afield as Australia and New York. Sören shook his head resignedly. He had no idea how he was ever going to accommodate so many. Nor was he sure whether he would forgive the Jarlsdottir this latest bombshell.

When she had first broached the topic last month, the gathering was to have been a "simple" moot. No problem. The traditional gathering of the Fenrir warrior-band would normally only have saddled him with about a fortnight of extra work in preparations. Maybe about half that in clean-up.

Accordingly, he had marshaled his regiments of hunters and cooks. He had laid in a supply of provisions that might bring a besieged army safely through a cruel winter. He had lined one entire wall of the House of the Spearsreach with barrels of ale, stacking one upon its brother's shoulders until they brushed the rafters. He had commandeered quarters to accommodate a few dozen visiting Fenrir shield-brethren.

This last was, in itself, no mean feat. Among the Fenrir, lives were short, but memories were long. On each previous occasion, the enthusiasms of the riotous warband had necessitated the complete rebuilding of at least one longhouse from the foundation up.

A streak of gray fur tore toward him across the Aeld Baile. Even as it bounded, the cub was already shifting. The runner skidded to a halt, nearly tumbling at the Hospitaler's feet, the tangle of human arms and legs ill-suited to the momentum of traveling at such speed on all fours. "Sören," the cub panted. "Must come at once. Storm-eye. The Talon. She says…"

Sören rolled his eyes. "Look, I've told you. She doesn't have to stay in any 'wyrm-ridden homid-den'. She can bed down in the woods for all I care. Hell, I've already put all of our hunters out of their own halls to fend for themselves within the treeline. It's all I can do just to try to find a place for everyone."

"Don't understand," the cub struggled to catch his breath. "She's firing up the warrior-band. They're on their way already. To the Icehouse. They're going to kill the fosterling."

"And you came running to me? Damned fool cub! Get the Warder, now! I'm going for the Jarlsdottir. Tell Brand we'll meet him there. At the Icehouse. Go."

Sören was already turning, the whirlwind sweeping up the hill toward the House of the Spearsreach.

Chapter 5

The mob of Garou closed in upon the Icehouse with all the subtlety of the angry snap of a steel-jawed trap.

The solitary building lay at the farthest edge of the Fenrir encampment, along the banks of the Hammerfell. Far out of sight of the House of the Spearsreach. The logs of the building enclosed three sides only, opening to the east, facing into the caern's center. In summer, the structure offered some slight protection from the worst ravages of cold and driving sleet. During the long winters, it was not so generous.

The interior of the long, low building was dominated by the old forge. But its heart had grown cold, dead. No fire had been lit within it these three years. You could still pick out the depression in the packed earth floor where Thor's Anvil had once stood, before the coming of the Jarlsdottir.

Although the House of the Spearsreach was the caern's center, the Anvil was its heart. Legendary weapons had been forged upon it—the grand klaives of the mythic Fenrir heroes, the silver hammers of the tribe's greatest law-speakers. To hear the skalds tell it, the Anvil was not made by mortal hands at all, but rather had fallen from the heavens like a cast of Thor's own hammer gone wide and missed its mark. They said that the noise of that impact was what had first summoned the sept founder, Ulfwain Klaivefather, over the blinding ice floe to this remote spot. And that all during the early days of the sept, while he was still Master of the Forge, never was there a fire stoked within. For in those days, the Anvil itself blazed with an inner fire—so much so that no man might hope to set hand to it. Only the Klaivefather could abide even its proximity, and its heat burned that mountain of a man black as pitch and bald as a new-whelped pup.

The Anvil—or rather its remains—now crowned the Hill of Lamentations, and there were some who still blamed the Jarlsdottir. Neither forgetfulness nor forgiveness came easily to the Fenrir.

There was no hint of forgiveness in the eyes of the mob that descended upon the Icehouse. They had heard of the ill-treatment their shield-brother, Arne Wyrmsbane, had received at the hands of their supposed allies, the Sept of the Dawn. Their intent was clear—to avenge that wrong without further delay.

The Icehouse had lain empty and untenanted since the Jarlsdottir's return. That is, until the coming of the fosterling. What the newcomer could have possibly seen in this inhospitable spot was anyone's guess, but he seemed to take an immediate liking to it. Within a week of his arrival, he had petitioned the Jarlsdottir and been granted permission to take up residence.

Up until that point, only the cellars of the Icehouse were used with any regularity. The walls, floor—even the ceiling—of the cellars were solid sheets of ice. At some time in the distant past, they had been lined with thick blocks of ice and scoured flat and seamless with heat and elbow grease. In this clime, there was no fear of their ever thawing or melting.

Cured meats hung from the ceiling. Barrels of small sour apples filled one corner and squat casks of hard cider lined the rear wall. Upon taking up residence, Cries Havoc had seen no reason to alter any of these arrangements. He moved directly into the basement among the bountiful provisions and became self-appointed cellarer and storemaster.

The wind howled down the rough-cut steps that descended from the center of the Icehouse. There had once been a double wooden door that could be pulled shut over the steps to keep any wildlife from straying into the cellars. Cries Havoc had had the doors removed shortly after taking up residence, immediately following the first time one of the cubs had placed a stout wooden rod through both door handles as a prank, sealing the newcomer within. Karin had found him only a few hours later. No harm done, but a point had been made.

Now, only the great bulk of the Warder blocked the doorway. "We have come for the fosterling!" Aeric Bleeds-Only-Ice thundered. "Join us or stand aside. There is a place of honor for you here, at the head of our column. It is time we put an end to this ill-considered exchange of peace hostages."

There was hearty agreement from the crowd at his back. Then one voice, female, pitched low to carry, broke from the uproar. "Peace hostages?" it challenged in the wolf-tongue. "More like hostage pieces! The wyrm-eaten corpse of your shield-brother! You have seen it. The way these Gaians treat with their allies. With claws hidden, cupped to their palms. You have seen it. The way we treat with such false-friends. That we will show them!"

The sleek she-wolf pressed forward through the angry mass of Garou. They parted around her as if she were a rock midstream. The patch of red fur at her throat blazed like a raw wound against the blinding glare of the snowfield. Her left eye was sealed, scarred, gazing no longer upon this world but upon the next. The Talons called her Storm-Eye and even their fiercest warriors did not dare to stare into the places she stared.

"No one enters this house." That was the Warder's voice. It was flat, threatening, little more than a rumble, a hint of distant thunder, a storm gathering. He stood just under the eaves of the Icehouse. Protectively. The cellar stairs were at his back. "The prisoner is not allowed any visitors."

"I meant what I said," Aeric replied. "Your place is here, Warder, at our head. You, more than any, has been wronged by this treachery. If you demand the kill, you will have it. It is your right. The bloodprice! Only let us be about it. Far better to present the Jarlsdottir with a vengeance already enacted than one in mid-course."

"There will be no vengeance this day, Aeric. The fosterling will pay, make no mistake. The day of his death has already been set. Tonight we will open the Concolation. The Gaian will appear before the Jarlsdottir for judgment two nights hence. He will stand before the tribes and the crimes of his sept will be recounted before all. And then—and only then—will we have our bloodprice."

Aeric Bleeds-Only-Ice made to protest, but a voice from just over his shoulder cut him off. "Speak in the ancient tongue!"

Storm-Eye snapped at the Warder. "This homid yelping is water-weak. Unfit for fighting. Good only for scratching at graves. The wolf tongue has claws. Use it or go back to digging in dirt."

The Warder did not so much as deign to glance in her direction. Holding Aeric's eye, he said pointedly, in the wolf-tongue: "None will pass within. I have spoken it. It is done. Two nights only we wait. There is time and always time. The pack will stalk this prey a while longer. Go."

Aeric bristled. He also had spoken, giving voice to the will of all here assembled—that the fosterling be put to death without delay. To back down now would be to invite shame and ridicule. He realized, for the first time, his true predicament. He was caught firmly between two rivals—Brand Garmson and Storm-Eye—each greater than himself. He was merely a knife-blade for these two antagonists to grapple over, each hoping to turn him to eviscerate the other. Nothing more.

Very well, he thought resignedly. *If I am to be a knife, I will at least be a keen one.*

His vision glazed over with a thin film of blood, coloring all before him as he forced his gaze to focus on the Warder. He growled his challenge.

Chapter 6

For the third time, Cries Havoc rechecked the latest provisions order from Sören Hospitaler. The last-minute procurement for this evening's feast. He was nervous, distracted. He muttered aloud as he read: *Venison, one and one side. Kids, three. Malum (barrel) one. Cider (casks) seven…*

It was no good. He stared blankly at the mound of provender. He could not seem to keep track of which items he had already checked off this time through the list—as opposed to the previous two times. He could hear the growing commotion above. He was under no illusions as to its nature. It was certainly not the arrival of the sledge to port all of this bounty up to the House of the Spearsreach. Sören had probably only given him this latest order to help keep his mind off more weighty concerns. He meant well. Cries Havoc doubted there would even be any sledge or, if there were, that he would still be around to greet it.

The sound of claws scrabbling for purchase on the icy floor brought him around suddenly. It was not the presence of uninvited guests that took him by surprise, but rather the direction from which the intruder came. The cellars had only one point of ingress—down the rough-cut stairs from the forge. It was the rear wall, however, that Cries Havoc now wheeled to face—a wall of unbroken ice.

A stranger stood there, enigmatic, smiling back at him. He wore a gleaming, predatory grin that seemed almost too wide for his face. Cries Havoc was acutely aware that the face behind that grin was neither wolf nor human—but something else altogether. The visage of a jackal.

The newcomer was a veritable visitation from the grave. It stood erect on two legs, its fur the shade of the night sky and its eyes ablaze like ice-blue stars. Cries Havoc had no doubt that this apparition, stepping unconcernedly *through* the wall of his house (which was, itself, already buried beneath several yards of solidly packed and frozen earth) had come to herald his death and usher him across that Final Threshold.

Cries Havoc watched the newcomer with rapt attention. Captivated. Waiting for what he knew must come, the first graceful movement of the attack, of his death descending upon him. Still he flinched when it came, and he had time enough to curse himself for his weakness.

But the raised hand fell, not upon Cries Havoc, but upon the stranger's own shoulder. Distractedly, he brushed at the ice crystals clinging to the fur of his arms and shivered. "I am Mephi Faster-than-Death. A friend. You must hurry, there is not much time."

So saying, he turned back toward the wall of ice. He leaned in close and breathed upon it, long and slow. Its surface fogged over. Rubbing a cleared circle with one hand, Mephi nodded, satisfied. The rough oval gleamed like a mirror. Only then did he notice that Cries Havoc had not moved.

The fosterling seemed rooted to the spot. He was shaking his head slowly and sadly. Mephi caught himself staring at the pronounced ram's horns that protruded from the cub's forehead, and flicked his gaze away quickly. Gawking at the boy's deformity would not put him at ease. He took advantage of the awkward pause to check the stairway. There was still no sign of the mob descending, but the obvious commotion above was rising in volume, pressing closer. He held out one paw toward Cries Havoc. "Come."

The fosterling shook his head again, more vigorously, with growing certainty. "No. You don't understand. I can't. I'm not going anywhere."

A flicker of impatience flickered across Mephi's features. "Listen, cub, there is nothing to fear. Nothing, that is, if we leave quickly. But any delay at this point may prove decisive. Please." He gestured toward the wall.

"No. This is my home now. Whatever might come, I will face it here," Cries Havoc said.

"Perhaps you do not understand what will come. They are here already, your accusers. I saw them on their way here, and a vengeance runs beside them. If they find you, it will not go well with you."

"There is nothing they can do to harm me."

"There is no one here to protect you from them," Mephi replied in growing frustration. "They will not draw back for fear of the Jarlsdottir. They believe they are serving justice and acting upon the will of the tribe. You are too far from your kin, and your enemies are within a whisper's-reach. We must go now."

"I have no enemies here," Cries Havoc replied stubbornly. "These *are* my people now. The Dawntreader entrusted me to the care of Karin Jarlsdottir. And he entrusted me *with* her care. I am bound to her. I will serve her until she instructs me otherwise."

"They will kill you," Mephi said slowly.

"Then I will die. I am ready to die."

"There are others who are not so ready for you to die," the jackal barked, losing patience. "If you will not flee this place for your own sake, then you will do so for the sake of your people. And for the sake of peace between the septs. What do you think will happen once you are so bravely dead? Once it becomes known that the Fenrir have executed a Gaian fosterling—and one who was innocent of any personal wrong-doing? Your people—your *real* people—cannot ignore such an affront. There will be more bloodshed. You may rely upon that."

"To the Fenrir, I am a peace hostage," Cries Havoc shrugged. "I will die to keep that peace. That is my duty and the *only* way to preserve the peace between the septs. Do you think I have not turned this matter over a hundred times already?"

He drew closer to Mephi and placed a hand upon his shoulder. As the jackal started to protest, Cries Havoc pressed on. "I thank you for what you came here to do, Mephi Faster-than-Death. It was nobly done and should not be forgotten. But I do not think it likely that I will be the one to sing this tale. I will not flee with you. When I am gone, you must find another storyteller to give voice to what was done here. Honor a dying man's wish. Do this for my sake."

There was an unmistakable growl of challenge from above. Mephi's eyes flicked nervously to the stairs and then back again.

"I could force you to come with me," he said speculatively. His voice was hushed. His ears pivoted, straining to catch the telltale sounds of the struggle above. "It would be a little enough thing. No, there is no sense in getting your hackles up. I would not have to subdue you, or even lay a hand on you. It would just be a matter of *hooking* you, like this, and then stepping sideways through the reflection in the polished ice."

Cries Havoc felt the sudden tug. It was as if a fist had clenched within his gut. The force jerked him up; he rocked forward onto the balls of his feet and flailed to catch his balance. It felt like being hauled upward by a rope anchored around his stomach.

"If you do not release me—immediately—I will ensure that your part in this black business becomes known before their fangs drag me down," he gasped around the struggle with his invisible tether. He might as well have been struggling against the tides. He was firmly and deftly hooked.

"But I will not take you so," Mephi concluded at last, seemingly oblivious to both the fosterling's protest and his threat. As suddenly as the pressure had come, it was gone again, nearly precipitating Cries Havoc to the floor. Mephi made no move to assist him, but continued speaking, his eyes straying back to the stairway. "I see that I am too late. Your death has overtaken you already, and you will not budge yourself to evade or even delay its coming. Stay then, if you long so for that moldering embrace. Goodbye, fosterling." He reached out one hand to touch the smooth, cool surface of the ice.

"Goodbye, Mephi Death-Follows-After."

The jackal stopped and turned slowly toward the cub. There was a great crashing above and a howl of pain and defeat. Then, the unmistakable sound of footfalls on the stairs.

Chapter 7

The Warder stood his ground as the younger warrior shifted. Aeric bellowed, the muscles of his back, neck and arms twisting and knotting, trying to tear their way free of the prison of human flesh. He towered over the Warder. Brand held steadily to Aeric's eyes as the other swelled to mountainous proportions. Seven, eight, nine feet in height.

The crowd pressed forward eagerly, as if already scenting the blood that must surely follow. They formed a tight cordon around the two antagonists. The nearest were actually under the eaves of the Ice House, but none made any move toward the central stair. There was a propriety to these things, a way of fang and claw more ancient and primal than any formalized human code. Aeric had challenged the Warder for the right to be the first down that hole—to personally drag forth their prey. None here would usurp that privilege.

At least, not until the outcome of that challenge was determined. They circled patiently, intent for the first sign of weakness.

Each of the two combatants felt that ring pressing upon him, felt the heat of body and breath. Each was fully aware of its significance. There was a danger to so public a challenge—to giving free reign to the bestial, and courting the same from the volatile mob. Once the blood began to flow, there would be no turning back.

Once the growling cordon caught the scent of falling lifes-blood, the stakes would increase dramatically. If either opponent were to so much as lose his footing or be knocked to the ground, that would be the end of it. The others—all the others—would be upon him in an instant. There would be no second chance to press or defend his claim under the flurry of claws and the crushing weight of bodies. Its verdicts were absolute and unappealable.

Aeric leaned over the Warder and bellowed again, directly down into his face. Brand's hair blew back from the force of it, but he neither shifted nor took up a fighting stance. He merely held the younger Garou's eyes.

There were yaps of impatience from the crowd. One familiar voice, bolder than the rest, taunted, "Look how the Warder cowers before him! Where is your rage, Warder? Perhaps the Jarlsdottir has not let him have his claws today. Maybe someone should run back to her homid-den and ask her for them."

If there were barks of derisive laughter from the circle, no one made any move to break away. If anything, they pressed all the more closely. Some could no longer hold to their human form but, wearing their wolf-skins, leapt in anticipation.

"Show your claws!" Aeric hollered. "You fight, or I gut you where you stand! You think I will not rend your man-pelt? You are a fool. If you will not fight, I will sharpen my claws with your bones. Face me!"

The Warder bristled under these insults, but still he did not move. Those who crowded him most closely might have seen a ripple pass along the muscles of his back and shoulders—the only outward sign of the slow, roiling rage within.

"You see him!" Aeric called to the onlookers. "He will not fight! He is no Warder. He is no alpha. He is no Fenrir. I tell you a final time, little man, move aside or I will cut you down. I can no longer stand the urine-stench of your shame and fear."

It was not a human sound that issued forth from the Warder's throat, nor exactly was it something animal. It was a howl, certainly, but no howl that had ever escaped a living, vibrant creature. It was a bellow of stagnant air from the grave, a mournful sound of racking pain and loss. All who heard it instinctively shrank back, thinking of loved ones and shield-brothers who had been taken from them.

The Warder did not change form, but something about him changed. Something rose up within him. A dark thing. A thing not entirely of this world. His grief unfurled from his shoulders like wings of purest shadow, and rose towering above him. Eight, nine, ten feet in height. It was a terror to behold. The shadow wore the *berserke* warrior-form like a shabby and ill-fitting garment—one that would not quite stretch to cover wrists and ankles.

Hunched over, the tattered beast shambled forward, bent nearly double, as if the ceiling of the Ice House were too low to encompass it. Its claws, each as long as a scythe, dragged the ground beside it with the grating sound of a whetstone at work. All of the creature's fur stood straight out on end, as if it were armored head to toe in cruel knives.

The shadow eclipsed the Warder entirely. He was a frail, pallid, fleshy thing, borne along before the wave of his own pain and grief. Any moment now, the shadow would crash over him, bear him down, drown him.

Aeric paled before this apparition. But he did honor to his name and to his kin. He launched himself directly, instinctively, for the beast's throat.

The crowd craned closer, straining after him, setting their teeth vicariously against the impact.

But Aeric's jaws never found that shadowy throat. A monstrous claw came up quicker than thought, catching him with a backhanded blow that spun him around in midair, sent him sprawling. The force of that blow resounded like a thunderclap. The very walls of the Ice House trembled in reverberation.

Aeric crashed through the ring of watchers, accompanied by yelps of pain and surprise. He landed heavily upon one shoulder and skidded across the ice, which was probably the only thing that saved him. By the time he came to rest, he had slid far enough from the ravenous onlookers that he had the briefest of moments in which to regain his feet. A howl of frustration went up from the assembled mob to see that he had escaped them, but they parted before him and held their claws as Aeric stumblingly hurled himself forward once again.

This time, he aimed his charge lower—not at the shadowy throat that towered above, but at the frail human form of the Warder below.

Seeing this new stratagem, a roar of encouragement went up

from the crowd. Those with weapons beat them upon shields. Those who wore lupine form leapt in anticipation. There was little doubt how such a confrontation must end. There was not one among them who had not felt paper-thin human flesh rend and bone shatter before such an onslaught. In their gleaming eyes the Warder was a corpse already, like the stag who, mortally wounded, would yet take two or three tentative stumbling steps forward before resigning itself to that fact and surrendering to the pull of the Earth.

Aeric was already inside the guard of the shadowbeast before the Warder could react. Seeing this doom descending upon him, claws extended and fangs gnashing, the Warder at last stirred from the depths of his own grief and loss. He had no time to think, to plan, to reason. Instinctively he pivoted, and one hand shot up before his face.

It was no defensive gesture, but a punch launched, with all the strength his human form could muster, directly into the face of death.

It was a futile effort and everyone, including the Warder, must have known it. But it was an act of indomitable spirit. And there is something in any place of power that stirs in the presence of an act of indomitable spirit.

Aeric felt the great fist of the shadowbeast shoot past him, just above his head—mirroring exactly the Warder's own movement. He saw the little man pivot and twist between the outstretched claws and heard the crowd's anxious rustling as it crouched, tensed to spring.

And then the pair crashed together with the sickening crunch of bones breaking. The more impressionable among the onlookers would later report hearing a sound not unlike the ringing of a silver hammer falling upon an anvil.

Aeric lay still, stretched full out upon the floor of the Ice House as if dead.

The cordon of watchers was too stunned even to set upon the fallen challenger. The predatory rage had drained from them as if they had suddenly fallen through the crust of an icy lake. They could only look on mutely as the Warder knelt over the body.

The hulking shadow of his grief rose up as if to strike the final blow, but then wavered. It turned and regarded its own upraised fist. The claws had grown hazy and out of focus; the lines of hand lost definition about their edges, dissolving into a fine mist. The inky shadowstuff smeared and then ran, gently pattering down upon the body of the felled hero.

It was a long while before anyone stirred or even breathed. They crouched in silence, muzzles lowered, hushed and expectant. The only sound in the stillness was that of the Warder's grief which, once given its head, could no longer be held at bay. He cradled the body in his arms as if it were that of his own son. Then, straightening, he turned his back upon them and vanished into the shadowed recesses of the Ice House.

Many milled around aimlessly a while longer, emptied of their vengeance and purpose, each privately wondering at the ambiguous miracle they had been called to witness. When Sören and the Jarlsdottir arrived, they found them there still and dispersed them back to their appointed quarters. No one seemed much inclined to give any account of what had transpired there.

Chapter 8

At the sound of heavy footsteps on the stair, Cries Havoc drew a steadying breath, straightened to his full height, and strode boldly forward to intercept his executioner. Mephi shook his head at the young fosterling's determination to meet his death here, on his own terms, in his adopted home. Cursing himself for a fool, he stepped forward at Cries Havoc's shoulder, remaining just a step behind. Presenting a united front.

Mephi was fully prepared for the appearance of a ravening Fenrir warrior, for carnage, for bloodshed. He took some momentary comfort in the fact that there was obviously only one person on the stair. Between the two of them, he and the fosterling might hope to subdue a solitary opponent. Perhaps faced with the reality of what his adopted neighbors had in store for him, Cries Havoc would come to his senses, accept Mephi's assistance, and flee this place.

What he did not expect was the Warder, saddened, humbled, and carrying a body in his arms.

Reaching the foot of the stairs, the Warder regarded them curiously. Deeply absorbed in his own thoughts, he was obviously aware that something was out of place, but he had too much on his mind to put a finger on it at that moment.

"You had visitors," he said, addressing Cries Havoc. "I sent them away." His eye fell upon Mephi and his expression hardened, some measure of the fog seeming to roll back from his gaze.

Mephi turned his hands palm outward, as if to make certain the Warder saw that his claws were sheathed and he bore no weapons. He backed away a pace and bowed. "I see that my presence here is not necessary after all. I thought only to warn the fosterling that he had guests. Had I known that you would intercept them *en route*, I would have saved myself the trip."

He laid a hand reassuringly on Cries Havoc's shoulder. "I will take my leave of you now. If you would speak further, only call for me. I will be near at hand."

Without a backward glance toward the ice wall, Mephi departed the chamber through a more mundane means, carefully stepping around the bulk of the Warder and ascending the stair.

"Thank you, Mephi Faster-than-Death" Cries Havoc called after him. The other turned on the stair.

"For what, fosterling? I have done nothing."

"For waiting with me," Cries Havoc said.

Mephi nodded. "Running, waiting, it is all the same at the end. But I do not envy you the waiting. I will come again."

While Mephi departed, the Warder laid the body out on the folding cot that served as Cries Havoc's bed. "There may be life in him still," he called over his shoulder. "But if there is, I cannot reach it. You will care for him."

"But Warder, I am no healer. And, unless I have greatly misjudged things, I will not be able to attend upon him long...."

The Warder turned and regarded him searchingly, for some sign of mockery or challenge. Satisfied, he grunted. "I could not leave him to the rabble. They would have turned upon him. And I would not have gone ten paces across the bawn with him before they were on me. Here is the only place."

"I don't understand," Cries Havoc said. "Why would you trust me with his life? They want to kill me. *You* want to kill me, from what Oksana has told me. Why do you think I will not just let him die?"

The Warder straightened and shrugged. "You will die, fosterling, for the death of my son. Have no fear on that count. But you will die in the proper time and in the proper place. You have three nights. Today I have fought, and may have killed, one of our finest warriors so that you might live to see that night. Do you understand me?"

A chill ran up Cries Havoc's spine. He could only nod in reply.

"Until that time, you will not leave this house. This is not the verdict of the Jarlsdottir, nor of the sept, but it is my ruling. I will do what is needful to keep you from harm until you are judged formally. Still you understand me?"

Cries Havoc found his voice. "Yes, Warder."

"By this ruling, I have taken from you your man-work. I know this. So I give you this chance." He gestured to the inert body. "If you can coax out his life, you will have done something worthwhile with the little time that remains to you. You will have returned to the sept one of her own and given Gaia back one of her champions. If you cannot, your efforts will be only a conversation between two dead men. A whispering between skulls. Nothing lost."

Cries Havoc was silent for a time. "I thank you, Warder. I will honor the gift you have given me. If there is life still in him, Gaia will have her champion."

Chapter 9

Nightfall on the ice floe. From the west, in the direction of the Hill of Lamentations, there was a thrumming in the air. The music of the moonbridges.

The entire sky glowed with the light of a dozen moons. Sharp shafts of moonlight crisscrossed the heavens. Each gleaming lunar pathway seemed to leap from the apex of the Hill, as if it might catch one of those moonglobes within its jaws. A fanfare of lights that would shame the aurora borealis streaked outward into the night sky, sounding its triumphant howl in denial of the vast impersonal interstellar distances. Calling the people together, calling them home.

But it was not the play of lights that captivated the attention, but rather the song. Just hearing that music, Sören seemed to shrug off ten years. His pulse and his step quickened in turn. The moonbridges sang, not to the ears, but to something more primal within each of the Garou. The music echoed within the secret chambers of the heart, it piped through the hollows of the bones, it snatched at the spirit like a strong wind catches an autumn leaf, sending it back skyward.

The song called to mystical side of the Garou, courted it, coaxed it out. It was a summons, a call to run, to leap, to dance. Those abandoning themselves to the communion of that song literally danced between the worlds. They chased over Umbral pathways, crossing the vast distances between the septs in a single evening.

Up ahead, from the House of the Spearsreach, there was a far different commotion—the sound of voices raised in heated debate. It was only with great reluctance that Sören turned toward this cacophony.

"It is preposterous. Blasphemous! Garou do not kill Garou." Oksana pronounced this phrase in a tone of reverence, as if reciting some ancient scripture or litany. Even drawn up to her full height, she looked very small and alone amidst the press of hulking Fenrir warriors seated around the High Table.

The hall groaned beneath the weight of the hastily constructed, rough-planked tables. Mountains of food rose from the board and rivers of drink wound their way down from the heights. The long benches were already packed shoulder to shoulder. Sören watched one visiting dignitary deftly rescue his dangerously canted plate from beneath a neighbor's elbow. He saw another take a dig to the ribs with somewhat less grace and somewhat more broken crockery. The resulting brawl seemed fairly localized, so Sören moved on toward the High Table, making a mental note to have the boys cobble together a few more replacement benches as insurance against similar outbreaks.

As crowded as the hall was, much of the assembly had perforce already spilled out onto the green. The throng of Garou milling about in the Aeld Baile would certainly result in fewer casualties among the furnishings, but if the crowd got excited, the possibility of structural damage to the surrounding longhouses was always a threat.

Sören tried in vain to tally up the total number of Garou present. There must be at least three score just within the House of the Spearsreach, not counting the mob out on the Aeld Baile. And he could not even hazard a guess as to the numbers of those who were present but had refrained from approaching the settlement too closely. Some cousins were more at home in the deeper primal woodlands than at any Jarl's table. Even within the clamor of the hall, Sören could make out the distant cries of their hunting and sporting—those who preferred the communion of the night to more civilized diversions.

And this is still the first night of the moot, the Master Hospitaler thought ruefully. The moonbridges would be thrumming throughout the night, and there was no telling how many more guests might have arrived by sunup.

It was the voice of Jotun Threeships that broke in upon Sören's musings. The Jarl of the Sept of Plundered Crosses, Threeships enjoyed a hard-won reputation as the most rapacious raider in all the Fenrir warband. He was seldom to be found among the comforts of his own hall, even when the seasonal ice clamped down on his warfleet, locking his ships at anchor.

Most of Threeships's excursions to the Sept of the Anvil-Klaiven, however, had been peaceful ones. The Old Jarl, Karin's father, had graciously forgotten the few that were not, and the two grizzled veterans always sat side by side as equals and shield-brothers in his hall. Accordingly, Threeships was one of the few present who was entitled to wear his weapons within the House of the Spearsreach. His hulking two-bladed axe lay before him on the table, its edge glinting silver. From its haft trailed, not the loop of a coarse leather thong, but a faded and worn pink ribbon. A lady's favor of some bygone day.

He stood now, brandishing a joint of venison wrenched from Thijs's proud eighteen-pointer. The head of that fine specimen was the centerpiece of the High Table. Threeships spoke through the branching antlers to address Oksana.

"Fine words, shadowling. But where were your fiery ideals when your people betrayed my shield-brother to his death? Where was your good council? Do not attempt to teach us our ways in our own hall. Blood calls to blood. The fosterling's life is forfeit. He will die."

Sören skipped back, narrowly avoiding the nearest overturning bench. All around the room, people leapt to their feet, banged drinking horns and shouted down their neighbors. The more ambitious lustily set about doing all three at once.

Oksana stood her ground and weathered the storm. When the worst of the clamor had died down to a roar, she spoke. "This is the way of the proud Fenrir? Garou killing their cubs? Eating their own young? This is the Wyrm-way. The Devourer rejoices to see his age-old foe, the mighty Fenrir, fallen into such desperate and self-destructive folly."

Some who were nearby made to lay hands upon her for her effrontery, but the Warder was instantly on his feet and between them. "Stand down," he growled. "Oksana Yahnivna is the guest of the Jarlsdottir; you will not lay hand upon her in this hall." He paused long enough to see Oksana bristle at this unasked-for rescue and then pressed on. "If you persist, I will not stand between you and her wrath. Your shame will be upon you twofold—once for your presumption and once for the beating you receive at her hands."

Oksana swallowed a heated reply and forced herself to remain composed as her antagonists, grumbling, settled back into their seats.

The Warder himself remained standing. His tone was casual, disarming. "No one here questions your familiarity—or that of your sept—with the ways of the Wyrm, Oksana Yahnivna."

His words were repeated the length of the hall accompanied by laughter and much banging of hands and tankards upon the tables. Before Oksana could object, he pressed on, "But you must, in return, accept our authority in the ways of the Fenrir. Blood calls to blood. We will return to you your fosterling, have no doubt of that. The Fenrir honor their word and repay their debts in kind. You will carry home to Sergiy Dawntreader the body of his sister-son, just as you bore my son's body here to us."

"This is madness!" Oksana protested. "Arne died a hero's death, in honorable combat against the Wyrm. His blood is not upon the hands of the people of the Sept of the Dawn. We lived with Arne Wyrmsbane. We fought beside him. We share in your loss and mourn our fallen friend." Oksana was nearly shouting now, to be heard over the din. "That there is a bloodprice to be exacted, there can be little doubt…"

At this, there were isolated shouts of "You see!" and "She admits it, by her own words!" and "Blood calls to blood!" But the hall quieted to hear what she would say.

"Yes, there is a bloodprice to pay. But it is the minions of the Wyrm that must pay the *wergild*. I have consulted with the Dawntreader in this matter and he has pledged ten of our fiercest warriors to fight side by side with the Fenrir to exact this vengeance. Some here will have heard tell of Gaia's Cudgel and their victories among the caverns of the balefires. You know this to be no idle pledge."

At that name, a renewed murmuring ran through the assembly. They had heard the stories, of course, about the warrior arm of the normally peace-loving Children of Gaia. Tales of these fierce hawks among the dovecote were largely hushed up by the Gaians, who considered such overt means of resolving problems as something of an embarrassment. Oksana knew that, among the Fenrir, things would be seen a bit differently.

It was some time before any one voice raised itself above the crowd. "Where are these fierce warriors?" Threeships asked skeptically, gaining confidence as his question was taken up by others in the crowd. "Why are they not here to pledge themselves in person, with their own oaths? Why do they not come forward to honor our dead? Why do they not join us in open contest, that we might test their mettle and see whether these tales are true? Where, for that matter, is the Dawntreader? Surely it does him no honor to remain skulking among the skirts of his women when there are rumblings of war."

"The word of Oksana Yahnivna is not in doubt." The new voice was calm, but it carried the unmistakable note of command. All eyes turned to the figure seated at the Jarlsdottir's right hand. A powerful man with features that might have been chiseled out of a rocky crag face by lightning-strike, and a lustrous mane of silver-white hair. The trappings of his armor were of red gold; his weapons, of purest silver. No one would have presumed to question the Margrave Yuri Konietzko's right to bear his arms within the hall. Few could so much as picture him without them. They were an essential part of the man.

The Margrave looked very much at home here among the battle-hardened Fenrir and their harsh northern wastes. He was no stranger to the worst ravages of nature or the battlefield. But he would have looked equally at ease among the luxurious decadence of the Shadow Courts. He was a born leader of men; for him, both armed encampment and palace were just backdrops to mirror and magnify his physical presence. He had a way of commandeering a room.

"Nor is the word of Sergiy Dawntreader," the Margrave continued. "Who, I understand, will be joining us shortly." He looked to Oksana and she nodded in confirmation. Dawntreader would have been on hand from the first, had not Oksana counseled patience and caution. She had feared that the abrupt

Gaian warrior and his promised troop contingent arriving *en masse* just might set off the political powder keg.

The Margrave continued. "The Sept of the Dawn has offered to pay this bloodprice—pledged the lives of ten of their finest warriors against this fallen one. It seems a conciliatory and heart-felt gesture—one motivated, not out of their being responsible for the Wyrmsbane's death, but out of a deep respect and, I believe, affection for him. There are battles at hand even now—critical battles—in which such a force would mean the difference between victory and watching as yet another caern is burned, pillaged and defiled. Know that there are those in this hall who envy you such an offer. With ten such warriors I could save two score Garou lives that will otherwise be lost before First Thaw."

It was no idle boast and there was not a soul in the hall who could not hear the truth and the pathos in his words. *Already he mourns for them*, Sören thought. *He spends his every waking hour among his dead.* Sören could picture the Margrave moving through his silent encampment, laying a hand on a shoulder here, confiding a word of encouragement there; telling a joke, asking about family back home, sharing a meal. He poured his strength into them, his dead, knowing they were lost to him already. He drilled them, marched them across vast distances, and led them howling into the teeth of the enemy.

And he watched them die. Over and over again.

Even the most brilliant stratagem, the most decisive victory was snatched only at great cost. Maybe when the day was won and the camp struck, there was only one fewer warrior among them. But the Margrave knew that was one warrior he had cost Gaia for the Final Battle. A warrior that would not be replaced.

All the heroes who will fight in that Final Battle have already been born.

There would be no new cubs, no new champions for Gaia. The Garou were fighting a battle they could not win, a battle of inevitable attrition. The Margrave knew that; it was something he had to live with every day. Every time he led men into battle, he was acutely aware that he had just slashed the odds of his winning the next fight. And the next. And the next.

When he closed his eyes, the Margrave always dreamed the

same dream. He was standing in the midst of a great battle-field, alone. Flies buzzed angrily around him. He could hear the moans of the dying, smell the reek of blood curdling in the sun. And a great sadness washed over him and his eyes burned with shame and tears. Not for his fallen comrades. Nor for the battle that was lost. But because he had fought too long, and now there was no one left to protect.

Every hand that might yet strike a blow against the Wyrm must be preserved.

"We thank the Dawntreader and the Sept of the Dawn for this generous gift in the memory of our fallen brother." It was Karin's voice that broke the heavy silence. The Warder rose to protest, but she raised a hand, forestalling him. "I am inclined to agree with the Margrave in his interpretation of this gesture. It is not an atonement, but a gift—freely given—to honor our fallen shield-brother. In this spirit I accept it."

"And what of the bloodprice? What of the wrong that has been done me and my line?" The Warder's voice was a bellow of indignation. "What use have I for these alleged Gaian warriors?"

"That issue," Karin said calmly, "has yet to be addressed. But I will hear no more talk of vengeance this night. Tonight we come together to honor our dead. We will hear of Arne's life and his deeds and his death. There are those present who can give witness to all three. Once he is laid to Gaia's bosom, then perhaps I will hear more talk of bloodprice, but not before."

The Warder growled low and, slamming his goblet down upon the table, stormed from the hall. The crowd parted before him.

"There you are, Sören," Karin called, catching sight of the Hospitaler. "Give us a story, old skald. A story of the fierce Fenrir warband. We have had enough of contentions this night and are sorely in need of more pleasant diversion."

There was scattered grumbling from about the room, but the antagonists grudgingly returned to their seats. There would be time enough to settle these things properly before the moot drew to its close. Outside, in the open, under the watchful eye of Luna.

Sören smiled. "There are many new faces among us tonight, guests in this hall. It is only just that they know something of us and of how we came to be here, enjoying this fare. The House of the Spearsreach," Sören began.

Chapter 10

It was in the season of Floodtide, when the Hammerfell carries the great jagged blades of ice upon its back, down from the mountains of the Fist. I can see them still—the cubs, leaping and skidding from one ice shard to the next, each seeking to prove himself sure of foot and fearless. Each seeking to outdo his fellows.

Now, not a year goes by without some young pup catching an ankle midstream. But few ever do so as dramatically and determinedly as our young Arne Brandson. Oh, he struggled heroically enough upon finding himself snared. So fiercely, in fact, that he managed to overturn the ice floe. It was three miles downstream he was dragged, if it was an inch. Upside-down, kicking and sputtering and hollering all the way before he managed to claw his way back to shore. And the fool cub was back at it the next morn, broken ankle notwithstanding.

It was three times we fished him out that week. And it might have been more had the unseasonably warm weather not intervened. His father did his level best with the boy—in the end threatening to strap a boat anchor to the cub's back every time he left the house, but nothing seemed to dissuade him from his ambitions of acrobatic prowess.

It was warrior-work dragging him from the Hammerfell that last time. In the end, it was the Ember-Whisperer who finally managed to cut the lad free.

"And to this day," called a jovial voice from the vicinity of the fire, "the Warder has not forgiven me the loss of that anchor!"

Sören laughed with the rest of them and turned to the Warder. The latter shook his head and said very softly, "It was a good anchor." It was clear, however, that he was absorbed in memories and regrets of his own.

"That was in the year of the Black Snow," Sören continued. "When the writhings of the Wyrm breached the mountainside and belched forth a cloud of noxious breath that blotted out even the life-giving sun, blanketing the land in a shroud of ash and night. Many of you gathered here well remember those starless nights and can say whether or not these things are so."

There was a murmur of assent from around the hall and someone pressed another drink into the storyteller's hands.

"In that season, the Jarlsdottir was in her sixth year and her birthday fast approaching. So it was that we find her, a girl-child of nearly seven years, standing hands on hips in the center of the clamor of her father's hall. The Fenrir warband pressed her sorely on all sides—much as it does this night. Exchanging tall tales and fearsome blows. Dicing, playing at droughts, sketching out plans for daring raids in the moisture of the cup rings on the table.

Catching sight of his daughter, the Old Jarl called out to find out why she stood so stern against the assembled might of his warband.

"Your warband," she answered him straight away, "is nothing more than a great racket. I cannot even hear what Brynhilde Silverhair says for all their boasting." At this a few of the nearest warriors laughed heartily and others leaned in to hear why the little one invoked the name of the Shield Maiden.

"She hears the voice of the Valkyrie?" Cnute Breech-Render wondered aloud to his neighbor. "Tell us, girl, what does the Warrior-Maid tell you?"

"She tells me that in this hall she cannot hear herself think," the Jarlsdottir scolded. "She says we would do better among the gossipmongers and fishwives. What's a fishwife?"

There was gusty laughter all up and down the Jarl's board at this question. Threeships, seated at the Old Jarl's right hand, leaned over and asked in a whisper, "This girl, she truly holds council with the Valkyrie?"

"Oh, yes," the Old Jarl replied in an equally conspiratorial tone. "And sometimes she speaks with Fenrisulfer himself, and even with Stalker-at-the-End-of-Days."

Threeships eyes widened. "And they answer her? By the powers!

This girl-child of yours, she will be a guiding voice among our people. Why, we have not had a Bone-whisperer among us since..."

"They are her dolls," the Old Jarl confided with a wink.

Threeships's ears went bright red and then he roared with laughter. "Pah! The blood of the snow-hare runs in your veins, Three-Day-Stone. Is it any wonder that I will not allow my people to trade either goods, blows or insults with the Sept of the Anvil-Klaiven? There is no honor in being so ill-used. We would have burned your longhouses to the ground years ago if I did not think that when we returned home, we would find you comfortably installed in our own lodges. Here, let us see if the fruit falls far from the tree."

So saying, he called out to the Jarlsdottir, "Come here, girl, where we can see you better. That's fine. Do you tell me that the noise of your father's warriors is an offense to you and to the Brynhilde?"

She bent her head, as if realizing for the first time that she might have offended her father's guest. But peeking up from beneath her bangs to meet her father's eyes, she saw him wink.

"I do, sir," she continued with renewed determination. "I cannot for the life of me hear what she will have in her tea."

Threeships, ignoring the general uproar that greeted this pronouncement, nodded sagely. "Well that we can not have. If you will grant me the honor of championing you, I will set things right with this rabble immediately."

The Jarlsdottir looked nervous and more than slightly embarrassed. But she set her chin and strode up to him. Standing directly before that giant of a warrior, she looked very small indeed. Solemnly, she untied the pink ribbon from what would one day be her warrior-braid. Unbound, her hair fell all about her shoulders. "I have never had a champion before," she said quietly, not meeting his eyes. Hesitantly, she laid the ribbon across his huge palm and folded his fingers around it. "I place this matter in your hands, Jotun Threeships. I know you will not fail me."

Something in the catch of her voice, the innocence and unquestioning trust he heard in it, hit Threeships like a blow. He continued with his grandiloquent speech and gestures, but those who knew him best

might have detected that something subtle had changed. As he pushed
his chair back from the table, he nearly upset it. He dropped to one knee
before her. Even kneeling, he still towered over her. With exaggerated
gentleness, he took both her hands.

"You honor me, my lady. I will not fail you."

They were a curious pair, locked hand in hand. The coarse, moun-
tainous raider in his pantomime and the slight girl peering trustingly
up at him.

"Before the door of this hall," the Jarlsdottir said. "Upend
the cup upon the snow."

"What?" Threeships asked, shaking his head as if his
thoughts were coming back to him only slowly and from a great
distance.

"It is what the Brynhilde said. How she will take her tea. I
can hear her now. Thank you."

The hall had, indeed fallen quiet. The Jarlsdottir's head was
cocked to one side as if heeding distant voices of her own. "Let
its contents fall and burn like blood. And pray that I visit only
the house of your enemy this night."

Threeships realized that she was tugging at him, attempting to pull him to his feet. "Come on," she said. "And bring that
cup."

He rose, shaking his head, and scooped up his drinking
horn as she had commanded on his way toward the door.

Laughing at the sight of the tiny girl with giant in tow, several other guests followed them out into the snow.

As they emerged into the moonlight, the Jarlsdottir took the
cup from the unresisting Threeships and held it above her head
in both hands. She closed her eyes and in a loud clear voice she
recited, "Brynhilde, Ice-Maiden and Claw-Tempest, we keep the
old ways. Remember us.

"When you stood alone against the threescore and three, we
were the strength of your arm. Remember us.

"When you suffered the Dozen Mortal Wounds and your
blood returned falling to the snow, we were the children who
sprang from each droplet. Remember us.

"When they hung your pelt from the branches of the World

Tree, we were the ones who mourned you and sheltered beneath you. Remember us.

"Bless this hall, but shun it. Let morning find you red and sated among the lodges of our enemies."

So saying, she upended the cup, pouring out the libation upon the snow. Around her, the now-quiet crowd of onlookers followed her example, emptying cup, horn and tankard.

Threeships looked upon her with wonder and then turned to the Old Jarl. Three-Day-Stone was smiling broadly.

"Dolls indeed!" Threeships accused. "This girl speaks sooth—your hall is no fit place for such company as she keeps. You must allow me to make her a present and I will have none of your stony-faced objections. You yourself have told me it is to be her birthday soon. I will build her a house for her dolls."

The Old Jarl groaned aloud. He was all too familiar with Threeships's excesses. "No. If I were to agree to such foolishness, you would commandeer all of my warriors on the spot and set them to fumbling over nails and pots of paint and miniature furnishings. I wouldn't have a single hunter left to feed my people."

Threeships waved aside these concerns dismissively. "I'll bring down my own craftsmen then. I've seen your warriors attempting to wield a knife before. It is always entertaining, but seldom productive."

"No, thank you," the Old Jarl replied more firmly. "You think I have forgotten. What was it the last time? Some anniversary or another. And that ravenous horde of yours descended upon us until there could not have been one runt left behind to guard all the supposed treasures of the Sept of Plundered Crosses. It must have been a full moon later before we were finally rid of them all."

"That was your father's burial ship—as you well remember," Threeships huffed. "And this is a mere dollhouse."

The Old Jarl sighed and turned to his daughter. "Well, what have you to say? This old scoundrel would make you a present. It will likely be half a year before we're free of him and his band of pirates, but if you will stand accountable for them while they are here, I will assent."

The Jarlsdottir blushed and regarded her shoes. "I am honored, Jotun Threeships. I know your men would never do anything to embarrass me during your stay here. I welcome your gift."

Threeships was on his feet, smacking his hands together like a thunderclap. "You heard the girl, you old goat! A dollhouse she shall have. And what a dollhouse!" He began marshalling his forces. Soon both his own warriors and those of the Old Jarl were shooting from the hall on various scavenging missions. Three-Day-Stone threw up his hands in exasperation.

The next day, the Old Jarl managed to corner Threeships at his commandeered construction site. "You said dollhouse. There's enough timber here to build a modest village."

"Some of your cubs got a bit carried away," Threeships replied. "But no matter. We've made a fine start, don't you think?"

"No. It's way too big. You said dollhouse." He stretched out his arms to encompass a space about three feet square.

"It's a gift," Threeships replied looking hurt. "I'm certainly not giving your daughter any skimpy little dollhouse. What would people say?"

The Jarlsdottir, who had been directing the returning lumber crew, joined them.

"No bigger than her arm's reach," the Old Jarl said flatly.

Threeships turned to the Jarlsdottir with a look of supplication. "Can you do anything with him? He has given his permission and now he comes to haggle it back."

"I am not haggling, I'm…"

"All right then, her spear's reach," Threeships said. "No bigger than her spear's reach. To think, begrudging a little girl a simple little dollhouse!"

"Fine! Her spear's reach, but no bigger. And the rest of this lumber, stack it next to the Great Hall. Maybe we'll have the harshest winter in living memory and we can burn through some small fraction of it before First Thaw."

Threeships ignored him. "Run and fetch your spear," he told the Jarlsdottir. "And hurry back before the old miser finds something else to object to. Probably the color of the draperies."

The Jarlsdottir grinned from ear to ear as she retrieved her spear from where she had cached it behind the woodpile. With the butt end, she drew a line in the soft earth at her feet and toed up to it. She stood stock still, eyes squinting at something in the distance. Then she drew back her arm and threw.

The cast sped high, strong and true. There was a brief flurry of motion at the spot where it came to earth.

"Well done, girl!" Threeships laughed. "A proud cast, let's take its measure." Together they set off to retrieve the spear. The Old Jarl hurried after them.

There, pinned to the ground, was a winter hare.

Threeships slapped the Old Jarl on the back. "The girl has quite a reach. Now, there's no use standing there with your mouth open. I trust we'll have no more haggling out of you this day."

Three-Day-Stone just stood there, shaking his head, knowing he'd been beaten.

And the Jarlsdottir had her own house and she called it the Hall of the Spearsreach. And Jotun Threeships and his people ate like kings for the space of three full moon-cycles. It was the only time he ever got the better of Three-Day-Stone, but he seldom let the Old Jarl forget it.

Chapter 11

Mari slipped silent and unnoticed from the Hall of the Spearsreach. Victor Svorenko had risen to his feet and begun to relate his story of the death of Arne Wyrmsbane for the assembly. She had, of course, been briefed on the relevant details of that story before she had left the States and she decidedly did not want to be on hand when the tale drew to its close and conversation turned to Arkady.

She was all too familiar with Arkady and his dangerous flirtation with the minions of the Wyrm. During the quest for the Silver Crown, she had witnessed firsthand the fruits of that dark obsession. And, in the end, she had stood beside her packmate Albrecht, when he had made it clear that Arkady would no longer be welcome in Albrecht's domain.

She didn't know why Albrecht had held back from a more formal judgment, or even bloodshed, at that time. Something to do with that delicate Silver Fang honor, no doubt. Albrecht always seemed hard-hit by Arkady's failings. Come to think of it, they all did. An entire generation of noble Silver Fang cubs had grown up in Arkady's shadow. He was their best and brightest. Not in a dozen generations had the line bred so true as it had in Arkady. And it was no secret.

His pelt was the achingly true white of moonlight on snow. At their moots, the Fangs sang him as their best hope—the promised war leader to grapple with the Wyrm in these Final Nights; the foretold ruler that would pull the Silver Fangs out of their dreams of decadence and take up the reins of the Garou nation; a savior to redeem their blood.

Albrecht had always been something of a black sheep, so maybe he understood more keenly than most how the weight of his people's expectation could warp, or even break, a man. It was hard to say just what he felt now. They never talked about Arkady anymore, she and Albrecht. Never so much as mentioned his name if it could be at all avoided.

But with this latest news, the subject could no longer be avoided.

"You have to go," Mari had said. "They're all expecting you to be there. They've all heard the rumors; they'll want to know what really happened between you two."

"I'm not going," Albrecht had replied.

"You know for a fact that there is no turning back for him now. No redemption. Arkady will kill, betray a caern, even strike a bargain with the Black Spirals if he thinks it will suit his purpose. Now, because of him, a Fenrir fosterling is dead and there's a massacre brewing between the Get and the Gaians. Damn it, the Get are going to execute a fosterling. Execute him! Sacrifice him on the altar of their honor! And it's the wrong man—and you know it. Arkady should have been the one to die. I'm going to this moot to tell them so. And you're coming."

"I said, I'm not going," Albrecht growled. "And I forbid you to testify against Arkady. I won't be responsible for—"

"You *forbid* me?" Mari's tone made it very clear that he had crossed the line. "I think you're forgetting who you're talking to. I'm not one of your subjects. And if you think for one minute that just because you're now High King of rural Vermont or whatever that I won't kick you around the yard until you remember who your friends are, you're fooling yourself."

"The topic's not open to debate," he said stiffly. "I don't want to see Arkady again. It was all I could do to keep from killing him last time. I don't know that I could manage it again."

That brought her up short. "So who's stopping you? He would kill you, you know. He's tried it before. So how about you just cut the crap and tell me what the deal is between the two of you."

Albrecht would not meet her eye. "Look, Mari, I can't keep you from going. But I won't have you denouncing Arkady. You show up there and they're all going to be looking at you, but it won't be your words they're listening to. They'll all be craning to hear in your words what I have to say. Even if I showed up there in person and told the bald truth about Arkady, then everybody listening would be thinking that it was just so much rhetoric in another Silver Fang feud. You speak out against him and it's worse. It's just some Silver Fang feud by proxy."

"It's not like that, Albrecht. They respect you. They'll listen to you."

He snorted. "Would they? Would they listen, I wonder, if I told them that Arkady was the best of us? The living embodiment of our blood. The end product of generations of our proud lineage. There will never be another like him, you know that. So much promise. Wasted."

A dark mood was upon him and he looked right through Mari as if not seeing her. "You have seen the fruit of this generation, Mari. The monstrosities birthed in the dark and locked away in attics and cellars. You are not deaf, you hear them howling through boarded-up windows when the moon is dark. What if I were to go to the Tribes, and I spoke the truth to them? That our people are dying. That all the cubs that will fight in the Final Battle have already been born. What if I told them that in passing judgment upon Arkady, they were passing judgment not only upon me, my tribe and my ancestors—but on all of us, all tribes, all ancestors? Arkady is the refutation of the Garou, nothing less. Of all we have strived for, of all we have achieved. If he has fallen to the Wyrm, what hope is there then for the rest of us, who are not, nor can ever be, his equal?"

In his words, Mari had felt the first tentative whisper-touch of Harano—the slow deep river of sorrow. She'd put an arm around him and spoke softly, hoping to help steer him back to shore.

But she honored his wishes. She did not speak out against Arkady, but rather slipped from the Hall of the Spearsreach and set her steps toward the Hill of Lamentation. There she had an appointment to keep.

Chapter 12

Mari pushed her way through the throng on the Aeld Baile and set off toward the Hill of Lamentations. Even from this distance, she could see the blaze of light from atop that hill where a dozen singing moonbridges converged. At the point of intersection, Thor's Anvil rang out as if struck by a resounding chorus of hammer blows, heralding each new arrival.

Sören had stationed a small but determined knot of young Fenrir upon the summit to welcome newcomers and to do their level best to find a place for everyone. These cubs were swelled with the pride and dignity of this responsibility. Many of their fellows would have to content themselves with standing thigh-deep in the snow just outside the House of the Spearsreach, craning to try to catch snatches of story, song and strategy that flickered out like firelight each time the doorway was opened.

In all fairness, it was no meager task. Mari felt comfortable that those on the hilltop would have enough to worry about without remarking upon one more late-night wanderer. Later, when the moon set, the hill would be crowded with those come to pay their last respects to the fallen Fenrir hero, Arne Wyrmsbane. But Mari's errand would be concluded well before then. She could take advantage of the solemn gathering to slip back into the crowd unobserved.

Had her mind been churning over less covert matters, she might have missed the fact that, as she passed the base of the hill and approached the Hammerfell, she had acquired a shadow.

She continued on as if unaware of her silent pursuer. But there could be little doubt now. It stopped when she stopped. And even here in the open, it was well out of sight whenever Mari cast about as if to make sure of her bearings.

If the presence of this tail disturbed Mari, she gave little outward sign of it. In fact, she smiled, hearing Albrecht's voice in her mind, raised in exasperation. About as useful as a second tail. *It was one of his favorite 'regal' pronouncements. Their packmate, Evan, had often found himself on the receiving end of this dismissive judgment—back when the cub was still finding his way and, more often than not, finding his way straight into trouble. It always felt funny going anywhere without her packmates, much less halfway around the world. It was a kind of empty, always-talking-to-yourself feeling. She wished they were here.*

This whole situation with Arkady and the fosterlings could flare up and really turn ugly at any time now. To tell the truth, it felt almost exactly like the kind of situation Evan used to drag them right into the middle of. It was also, not coincidentally, the kind of situation he had become so adept at disarming. Evan had a way of bringing people together when it counted, of putting differences into perspective.

Hell, she would have been grateful even to have Albrecht here right now. Volatile political situations were not his long suit but, when pushed, he had a knack of becoming far more volatile than the original problem. This usually brought matters to a head, at least. So far, she had seen no sign of Arkady. Maybe he wouldn't even show up. Maybe all of Albrecht's objections were groundless.

A shadowy form stepped out directly in front of Mari, startling her from her reverie. By way of greeting, it launched a powerful roundhouse kick at her head. Mari went low and barely slipped beneath it, her own leg sweeping out, seeking to knock her opponent's feet from under him. Distracted, she had not accounted for the icy surface, and she nearly toppled as she made contact. She caught herself, but one hand sank to the forearm in the loosely packed snow.

She was moving instantly, righting herself, spinning away. It was a good thing she did. The fierce downward kick that might have shattered her kneecap landed instead upon the soft flesh at the back of the knee. She went down again heavily, with a grunt, but without any broken bones to show for it.

Another strike, following hot on the heels of the last, whistled toward her head. Mari made no effort to roll out of the way or even to duck the blow. Both her arms came up, almost in slow motion. They came together for the briefest of instants, at the exact point where they intersected the path of the kick, and then her arms—almost effort-lessly—spread wide again, deflecting the force of the blow and hurling her opponent backwards.

He had barely skidded to a halt on the snow when he immediately leapt forward again. A flurry of punches, each too fast for the eye to follow, rained down upon her, each met by a blur of blocks and coun-ter-strikes. The flesh of Mari's hands and forearms stung from cold and impact. She tried to force herself to breathe slowly and shallowly between her teeth. Every gasp in the frozen air was a cloud that might obscure the true path of the next attack.

It was time to end it. If this went on any longer, the combatants would doubtless draw the attention of those on the hilltop. Being dis-covered here was not at all a part of Mari's plan.

Instead of blocking the next punch, she instead met it head on, her grip ensnaring her opponent's wrist. She brought her free had up in a lightning-fast swipe that would snap the joint. But the blow never fell. There was a second slap of flesh meeting flesh and the two antagonists found themselves locked together, fists firmly clasping wrists.

"You fight poorly in the snow, Mari Cabrah," said an almost feline voice pressed close to Mari's cheek.

"And you're about as stealthy as a steam train, Kelonoke Wildhair," Mari replied. "I could barely see you through the fog of all your panting and huffing. And what would you know about snow?"

"I know enough not to roll about in it. Look at your hands, they're as pink and raw as a newborn cub's!"

Mari could not help but look. Their hands were still locked together between their faces. She laughed and loosed her grip. The two embraced.

"It's good to see you," Mari whispered. And then added as an afterthought, "Even if you do fight like a man."

The brief struggle resumed among muffled threats and invectives. In the end, it was Mari's sharp whisper that called for the halt. "Enough! If we haven't been spotted already with all that snow you're kicking up, we will be shortly. I'm finding it hard to believe that you called me all the way here just so that I could thrash you about in the snow. What's this all about, and why all this cloak and dagger?"

Wildhair's eyes squinted toward the glare of the hilltop and after some study she snorted dismissively. "That lot hasn't seen a thing. Not surprising, standing in the middle of that light-show. But we'll move off a short way if that will make you feel better. I'm glad you came. It's getting so that I can't leave the caern any more without my movements being scrutinized. I'm afraid I've struck kind of a devil's bargain and now I've got to take advantage of what opportunities present themselves. Like this Concolation."

"Slow down, I don't understand anything you're saying. Scrutinized by who? And what's this about a devil's bargain? After this whole ghastly business with Arkady, I'm still a little sensitive about that topic."

"Not *that* kind of devil's bargain. Things are not so desperate as that. Well, not yet, anyway."

"Don't even joke about..."

"Sorry," Kelonoke attempted a disarming smile. It only gave her an even more manic aspect. She shrugged. "I guess things have been a bit rough on everyone lately."

"More trouble back at home?" Mari asked. "I've been catching bits and pieces on the news, but there's only a trickle. The networks have long since written off public interest in the latest atrocities coming out of Serbia and Bosnia."

As a tribe, the Black Furies traced their origins to ancient Greece. The fierce sisterhood of women-warriors was descended from the tradition of the Amazons and the Maenads. Even now that they were scattered across the globe, the Furies still looked upon Greece as the tribal homeland. Caerns like Kelonoke's Sept of Bygone Visions had attained something of the status of pilgrimage sites. Unfortunately, they were never far from the firing lines when troubles erupted in the Balkans.

"It's worse than ever," Kelonoke confided. "Your TV audiences aren't the only ones who have grown numb to it. The marauding rape gangs, the genital mutilation, it's all become commonplace, accepted, the status quo. These women—the victims!—look at you like you're sick for even suggesting that there's something wrong with what's going on there. How the hell are we supposed to help folks like that?"

Mari didn't have any answers to give her. "I know," she muttered. "I know. Sometimes it's got to feel like what's the point of even fighting if you can't win. If you can't even make a difference."

"And it's not the Wyrm that's doing this to them! Although you can believe the Wyrm is right there, feeding off all of this stupid, senseless suffering. It's not the Black Spirals and their twisted appetites and petty cruelties. It's not even the dumb fomori who don't know anything else but the rule of torment—giving it and receiving it. It's humans! Plain old everyday make-you-want-to-scream-and-scream humans. And you can kill them, kill them till the streets run red, but it won't stop. It just doesn't stop."

Mari quickened her pace to catch up and put an arm comfortingly around her shoulder, but Kelonoke shrugged her off. "You know the worst thing?" Wildhair pressed on. "They don't even care what you do to them. Kill them, torture them, beat them senseless, humiliate them. Because as soon as you turn your back, you know what? They're doing it to themselves. You might as well just stay home, because all you're doing is making it easier on them. Doing their dirty work for them. We're dying out there, Mari. And it just doesn't make any difference."

Mari drew a deep breath and tried another tack. "All right, how can I help?"

Kelonoke regarded her as if Mari had not listened to a thing she had said. "I don't know that you can."

"Then why did you ask me to meet you here? In this frozen uninhabitable corner of Norway…is this even Norway? Hell, I'd be surprised if anyone wanted to take credit for this place."

"Your countrymen planted a flag in Antarctica," Kelonoke reminded her sulkily. "And on the moon for that matter."

"All right! It's not about who owns what. It's not even about where in hell we are. I want to know why you asked me to meet you here. I thought—foolish flighty female that I am—from all this venting about the Balkan situation that *that* might have something to do with it. But apparently not. So spill it, or I'm going back right now and you can mope around out here in the snow to your heart's content."

The two regarded each other icily for a time. Kelonoke broke the silence. "I guess I'm not used to asking for help."

"You're not much good at it, that's for sure. I—"

"Shut up, Mari. Just listen a minute." She cleared her throat. "I want you to come home with me. To Greece. To the Sept of Bygone Visions. I want you to see what's going on there first-hand, with your own eyes."

"I don't understand. What good is that going to..." She caught Kelonoke's look and broke off abruptly. "Sorry, go ahead."

"If things here at this Concolation go as I fear they might, we're going to need somebody to speak for us back in the States. The Furies there have to know what's going on in Serbia. Someone needs to make them understand—understand that it's not just a little ethnic squabble half a world away. Promise me, Mari."

"Kelonoke, I..."

"Promise me!"

"All right, I'll come. But that's all I'm promising. After that you can come back with me, to the States. Your story will have much more impact coming from your own mouth than I could ever give it. Our sisters know you there. They will listen."

Kelonoke seemed not to hear anything Mari had to say beyond her promise to come to Greece. Wildhair's eyes had a faraway look as if apprehending dangers not yet made fully manifest in this world. "There's a wrong there, Mari. I don't know how to describe it. A wrong that goes deep, deeper than the detritus of years, back to the very beginning of things. It's had centuries to brood and grow fat upon the ceaseless warfare and hatred and brutality—and now it's stirring. It's shrugging off its mantle of blighted earth and caked blood. I had hoped not to live long enough to look upon its true visage."

"Don't talk like that." Mari suppressed a shudder and

punched Kelonoke in the arm. This seemed to bring her back to herself and she gave Mari a good-natured shove.

"You are as easily frightened as a rabbit, Mari Cabrah. Look how far we have wandered! Let us rejoin the others. Unless I mistake that fire upon the hillside, they are, even now, returning Arne Wyrmsbane to Gaia's bosom."

Turning, Mari could indeed see the flames of the funeral pyre straining skywards toward the delicate arcs of moonbridges. She wondered how many more of Gaia's champions would return to Her before Mari had fulfilled her promise and returned home again.

As the two Furies picked their way over the frozen ground back toward the Hill of Lamentations, a long, low howl tore free of the crowd of mourners on the hilltop. It swelled and rose to a haunting, keening wail. Mari felt it like a blow to the stomach. She saw Kelonoke leaning forward as if trying to make headway against a strong wind.

The cry was taken up by each of the patrols along the perimeter, passed along the lines like a summons to battle. It swelled in volume and intensity, echoed back from every point of the compass. Stragglers on the Aeld Baile heard it and, looking up, bared their throats to Luna, adding their voices to the dirge for the fallen hero. The wail caught like tinder and raced through even the heartwood where their wildest brethren ran, and not even a Garou dared be caught out wearing a human skin this night.

In this way, the Fenrir sang their shield-brother to his rest.

Chapter 13

The Warder, Brand Garmson, stalked the perimeter with visible impatience. Even his own pack gave him a wide berth. He did not so much patrol as churn up the earth. It was still a half hour before sundown and the formal reconvening of the moot.

Not that there had been any lack of festivities to fill the daylight hours. It seemed that Sören Hospitaler had put himself through unnecessary anxiety over accommodations; few of those present spent more than an hour or two in sleep. There was simply too much going on: old friends to catch up with, new ones to meet. Challenges to be issued and answered. News and stories changed hands like currency.

The Fenrir warband fell to its traditional feats of carnage with an enthusiasm proportional to the size and prestige of its unprecedented audience. They outdid themselves in free-for-all bouts of drinking, boasting, sparring, wrestling, climbing, hunting and hammer-throwing. They held footraces up and down the sheer sides of mountains and team races along the treacherous slope of an iceberg that had run aground nearby. The trick to this latter event seemed to be to reach the peak not so much as fast as possible, but rather without overbalancing and upending the whole. They competed at sword-breaking and shield-splitting and to see who could cut through the greatest thickness of ice with a single stroke of a war axe.

They swapped blows and stories with equal zeal until it became a test of endurance—to see who could endure the onslaught the longest and still give as good as he got. They greeted one another in the ancient manner, each seeking to outdo the other in the recitation of his deeds or the litany of his proud lineage.

The Warder, however, held himself rigidly apart. He passed the interminable daylight hours drilling and testing his patrols, probing for any hint of weakness—or worse, levity—and ruthlessly grinding it underfoot. There was an audible sigh of relief all along the perimeter when the Warder angrily announced that he would have to go and check on the prisoner. He was taking no chances on the fosterling having a sudden change of heart and attempting to flee.

It was not surprising then, that although the perimeter patrol did not know quite what to make of the strange party that approached the bawn shortly before sundown, they saw in it a welcome distraction. Jorn Gnaws-Steel went forward to meet the newcomers, his wide grin revealing the fact that no fewer than six teeth were missing along its upper right side. As the three figures drew nearer, however, the grin vanished. Jorn let out a low growl of warning that, although it had no discernible effect upon the approaching trio, did summon his packmates to his side.

The newcomers were cut of a single mold: short, stocky, powerfully built men. But their skin had an unsettling pallor to it—one usually associated with certain varieties of mushroom that grow only in the deep woodlands and shed a faint phosphorescent glow. The leader of the group bore a blackened iron spear, braced before him like a battle standard. The flutter of white dangling from its point was unmistakably the pelt of a white wolf.

"Hold your ground," Jorn growled. "State your name and your business here."

The leader tossed his macabre pennant disdainfully and one-handedly to the man on his right. He strode forward, ignoring Jorn's warning. "I am called Knife-between-Bones. These are my companions. We have come to address the moot. I hope we are not too late."

His voice had a strange undertone to it, like the squeaking of bats. It grated on the nerves. Jorn felt the muscles of his face bunching in answer to it, and he forced his features to relax.

"What sept are you from, Knife-between-Bones? And what do you mean by bringing this grisly trophy here?"

"Grisly trophy?" the newcomer seemed genuinely puzzled. He turned a questioning look upon his companions and then comprehension lit his features. "Oh, the white flag. It is usually considered a sign of truce or parley," he confided. "It means we have not come to kill you."

The man to his left snorted. From his expression, it was clear that he did not think much of this arrangement, but he was willing to humor his fellow for the present. He scratched distractedly at the flesh of his forearms. Where the skin peeked from his sleeves, it seemed mottled with sickly blue-green scabs. Jorn had the unsettling impression that these wounds formed some kind of pattern or sigil. They seemed to writhe and shift the longer he stared at them.

"Well, that is a relief," Jorn said, tearing his gaze away. He forced his lopsided three-quarters smile back to his face. "It's not exactly traditional to bring a spear to the parley, but we'll overlook that for now. You're not from around here, are you?"

"No, but it is kind of you to ask. You will take us to the assembly now please," Knife-Between-Bones said.

Jorn held up a hand. His voice was calm, with barely a waver of disbelief. "We'll have to announce you, of course. Can I tell them what this is about, or shall I just say that Knife-Between-Bones and a party of Black Spiral Dancers have arrived under a flag of truce?"

Knife-Between-Bones seemed to consider. "If you would be so kind, you might just say that the delegation from Lord Arkady is here. We would not like to set your cubs and womenfolk to flight. You have been most helpful. I will make a point of mentioning that to your superiors. "

"From Lord Arkady?" Jorn could not longer keep the note of incredulity from his voice. "You would have me believe that you are kinsmen of Lord Arkady?"

Knife-Between-Bones bristled with in indignation. "I am! Or rather, I was," he finished less certainly. "Things always become so muddled when family is involved, don't you agree? Nevertheless, we will address the assembly."

He advanced again, this time until his chest met the palm of Jorn's hand. The flesh gave slightly beneath the Fenrir's fingers.

Soft, wet, wriggling. His every instinct cried out for him to pull his hand away quickly, but he held his ground.

"You forget," Jorn said, bearing down on him with his gaze. "We must announce you first."

"Ah, yes." Knife-Between-Bones stepped back and turned to his retinue. "He says he will announce us," he repeated loudly.

Jorn wiped his hand off on his jeans while the other's back was turned. His skin still stung as if he had just drawn it out of a clump of nettles. He casually turned and addressed his nearest packmate in a whisper through clenched teeth. He could only offer a silent entreaty to Gaia that Fimbulwinter would realize the delicacy of this situation and not do something stupid.

"You will go to the Icehouse," Jorn told him. "And announce our guests. You will say that the delegation from Lord Arkady is here. Please stress to the Warder that we are keeping them waiting here. Do you understand?"

Fimbulwinter gave him a questioning look, as if to make sure that Jorn knew what he was doing. "Go," Jorn urged. His companion shook his head and then loped away across the bawn. Jorn turned back to the delegation.

"It will be a few minutes only. But I am curious, why hasn't Lord Arkady come himself? I would think that he would want to face his accusers personally...."

Distractedly, Knife-Between-Bones turned back to him. "What's that? Oh yes, you again. Lord Arkady regrets that he will be unable to join us. He has been...detained. But it is no matter, we will vouch for him."

He turned back to his colleagues, leaving Jorn to gape, slack-jawed at his audacity.

A grumbling at his ear brought Jorn back to himself. "The Warder comes," Fangs-First said. Before Jorn could turn to follow his packmate's gaze, the announcement was corroborated by a distant thundering of paws over the frozen ground.

Too soon! Jorn thought. *Tell me he didn't rush straight here. That he didn't come alone.*

He turned, already knowing what he would see. The Warder, in his hulking dire-wolf form, chewed up the open stretch of ground between them. Fimbulwinter pounded along furiously in his wake, but had already fallen a half dozen lengths behind. There was no other sign of movement—or reinforcement—along the bawn.

Jorn cursed under his breath and flashed a quick hand signal to Fangs-First. *Circle around right. Slowly.* The one with the leprous tattoos carved into his arms was the dangerous one, Jorn could tell at a glance. Edgy, spoiling for a fight.

By this point, even the visiting party had turned its attention toward the huge beast bearing down upon them. "Ah, here at last is someone with an appropriate sense of urgency come to take us before the assembly directly. Shall we go in now?"

Jorn ignored this question and interposed himself directly between the approaching freight train of the Warder and the delegation. He raised one hand, signaling for the Warder to halt, already knowing it to be a useless gesture. The Warder was not about to check his rush.

If he slowed at all, it was only to better time his spring.

"The flag of truce!" Jorn had time to bellow as the Warder pushed off the earth. Then Jorn was forced to fall flat in order to avoid the raking claws sailing overhead.

The Warder hit Knife-Between-Bones with the resounding crack of a felled tree crashing to the undergrowth. Jorn could not see the result of that impact—could not see the Spiral at all for that matter. The leader of the delegation was suddenly and totally eclipsed by the mass of bristling fur and fang. Then Jorn found that he had little attention to spare for anything but his own plight.

There was a great bellow of pain from Fangs-First and the acrid reek of charred fur. Jorn felt, rather than saw, the body of his packmate flying toward him. Even so, he barely managed to scramble out of its path and regain his feet. He was greeted by a scene straight out of nightmare.

The scabrous Spiral had shed its human form like a dried and ill-fitting skin. It stood revealed, sleek, moist and viscous, rearing like a cobra. Its rage-form was utterly devoid of fur, the veins standing out clearly through parchment-thin flesh. Jorn would not have taken it for the same creature at all were it not for the pulsing, blasphemous runes covering its arms. These now crackled with an eerie radioactive glow. The glyphs no longer seemed gouged into its skin, but rather they hovered just above the surface—sizzling with energy and giving off the unmistakable reek of ozone.

The beast stepped forward into the space recently vacated by Fangs-First. Out of the corner of his eye, Jorn could see his packmate sliding across the icy ground and spinning to a stop. He lay still and made no effort to get up again.

Not good. Jorn thought. *First fall to the visiting team.* He was already shifting, surrendering to the shuddering, racking, bone-popping contortions of the *berserke* warrior rage. Jorn felt the spark of self flicker and waver uncertainly before the rising tempest. The ground beneath him gaped wide as Gaia threw back her head and howled through him.

At the eye of that bellowing tempest, there was a moment of absolute, still clarity. Jorn could see each detail of the melee unfolding around him. He could see the individual sparks still chasing each other through the blackened fur of Fangs-First as he lay, living but unmoving, in the snow.

He could see Mars-Rising bearing down upon the foe from a position directly opposite Jorn's own. It was the right attack at precisely the wrong time. If it had come any earlier, it might have coincided with Fangs-First's bull rush, guaranteeing that one of them, at least, would have found his mark. If it had come later, Jorn could have launched an attack to monopolize their opponent's attention, leaving an opening that could be exploited. As it was, Jorn could already see the first hints of the Spiral's pivot—the turn of the foot, the slight shifting of the weight. Its right fist would intercept Mars-Rising in mid-leap.

Jorn could see Fimbulwinter plowing forward on all fours, head lowered. He shot arrow-straight and sure at the last of the delegates, the standard bearer. Jorn wanted to howl a warning to his packmate, but there was no time. Already he could see the cruel tip of the blackened iron boar spear dipping, coming into line. The white wolf pelt banner—the flag of truce—trailed the ground, sketching a shallow furrow in the snow.

At the center of the carnage stood the Warder, undaunted, caught in the midst of the change into his warrior-form. His left fist was buried past the wrist in abdomen of the leader of the delegation. The force of that blow had lifted Knife-Between-Bones from his feet and the Warder held him there, bellowing defiance up at his pinioned foe.

And all four of the Fenrir howls were one howl. Or perhaps they were only aspects of that One Howl—the cry of pain and outrage that echoed through the hollow places of the earth long before any of their births, which would resound long after even their names had been forgotten. The Fenrir were the Howl of Gaia. They were born into this world screaming their defiance; the steadfast were permitted to take their leave of it in the same indomitable spirit. It was the single defining act of their existence.

Then that single moment of clarity passed and time sped forward again, a blur of fang and claw. The Spiral's claws streaked out and caught Mars-Rising just beneath the jaw. Flesh rent; blood gushed. Even as the blow made contact, the sizzling glyphs of energy on his forearm snaked out and crashed down across Mars-Rising's head like the cracking of a whip. Fur burned and blackened. The blow felled him, laying him out crumpled at the feet of his antagonist. Mars-Rising had just enough strength left in him to roll aside before the next blow could fall. He rolled over and over, the packed snow extinguishing his burning fur. He clawed desperately at his own scalp where the fiery contagion had pierced flesh and now seared its way inward.

Seeing this deadly opponent in action, Jorn quickly changed tactics. The usual pack maneuver of circling the foe and then harrying him with lightning- quick in-and-out attacks from all directions was clearly not working here. Two packmates were down already and he was now facing a one-on-one fight at best. The howl of agony from Fimbulwinter told Jorn that his packmate had discovered his oversight and met with the boar spear. That didn't speak well for the odds. If Jorn were fortunate, the spear might at least break beneath Fimbulwinter's weight. Jorn didn't particularly relish the thought of being set upon from behind, but if it had to happen, it might at least be by a disarmed foe.

He decided to abandon prudence. The precise darting attack he had launched transformed suddenly into a ferocious all-out pounce. He desperately hoped that Mars-Rising had bought him enough time.

Jorn let out a bellow of triumph as he felt his claws pierce the crackly, paper-thin flesh and slip gratingly beneath the bones of one shoulder blade. Then his full weight crashed down upon the Spiral's back, driving him face-downward to the ground. The sickly tattoos writhed and sizzled as they were pressed into the snow. A hissing cloud of steam enveloped the two combatants. Then Jorn's fangs clamped down upon the back of the Spiral's neck and, with a toss of his head, hot blood splattered across the snow.

The Spiral tried to rise to his knees, shuddered, and lay still. As the steam cleared from before his eyes, Jorn could see the gleam of white bone amidst the wreckage of the other's throat. Its head was cocked at an unnatural angle, nearly torn clean from its body. The imprint of his own ragged grin, rendered in mirror-negative, smiled up at him.

The Warder held Knife-Between-Bones aloft by one hand. His fist was bunched within the Spiral's abdomen. The Warder watched as his claws and the force of gravity slowly rent his opponent from groin to ribcage.

Knife-Between-Bones disdainfully spat mingled blood and bile down into the Warder's face. From some inner reserve he managed to summon up the strength to speak, to curse his killer. His words came in broken gasps. "Yes, you have done well, my brother. Revel in my blood! You will make a fine champion for Malfeas. Already, you have passed the First Gyre of the Black Spiral...."

"Silence!" The Warder shook him, and a fit of coughing choked off the Spiral's words. Blood ran from the corner of his mouth. He smiled.

"There is no return, Brand Garmson. Yes, I know you. Your

name is already etched in Balefire into the walls of the Cave of Remembrance. I have seen it with my own eyes, run my fingers over your mark..."

The Warder felt a cat's-tongue caress running up his back and he shuddered.

"Yes! You know I speak truth. You will come to us in the end and willingly, once you realize what you have already become. You cry out for innocent blood. You strike down your own packmates. You attack strangers upon sight. You dishonor the flag of truce. You—"

The Warder could take this dark litany no longer. His left fist drove skyward, claws piercing heart and lungs indiscriminately. His right hand lashed out in a vicious swipe, raking across the abdomen and nearly bisecting Knife-for-Bones. Disdainfully, he cast the body away from him.

He turned toward his left, to the only figures still upright upon the field. Fimbulwinter stood pierced through the breast by the iron boar-spear standard. Its blackened shaft was scored with deep gleaming claw marks where he had tried to carve through the weapon or knock it from his foe's hands. Failing that, Fimbulwinter had set upon the only course of action left open to him, dragging himself—step by agonizing step—forward up the length of the spear. He had already closed half its length, but each footfall threatened to be his last.

The Warder bellowed his challenge. The Spiral caught sight of him and nearly lost his grip on the spear. It would be another moment still before he realized that his weapon had suddenly become a deadly liability—an anchor rooting him to one position. But that moment would be enough.

The Warder's spring caught the unfortunate spearman high on the chest, crushing collarbone and forcing him to the ground. It was over in a moment. The spearman lay dead and gutted. The Warder raised his red muzzle from the remains and howled victory and defiance. Outlying patrols streaking toward the combatants saw the Warder silhouetted there against the setting sun like the very embodiment of the Dire Wolf. The ragged specter of death.

But the vision was gone as quickly as it had come. They were fully aware that he was their Warder once more as he lashed into them, enumerating their failings in excruciating detail. In the first breath alone they were late, inattentive, out of shape and not at their assigned posts. The litany of their shortcomings did not stop at the first breath.

The Warder's sharp reprimands sent men scurrying to free Fimbulwinter and to bear him, along with Fangs-First and Mars-Rising, from the field.

It was only the warning growl from Jorn that brought the Warder's damning recitation up short. *Danger. Behind you. Spirals. The Dead.* A seasoned warrior could be amazingly articulate, conveying extensive information in one rumbling guttural note.

The Fenrir wheeled, falling instinctively into a loose skirmish line. Keen eyes cast about for the source of this new threat. It was the Warder who saw first and almost immediately he wished that he hadn't.

There was movement from where he had left the leader of the Spiral delegation. A stirring. The body of Knife-Between-Bones lay in the snow, nearly torn in two. But the body did not lie still. From the gaping hole at the base of its ribcage, something white and viscous writhed. It probed the air experimentally and, emboldened, snaked outward.

It swelled as it came, at first a mere tendril but soon growing as big around as a sapling. As the Warder looked on in mounting horror and revulsion, the tip of the squirming appendage split in two, each branching swelling to the thickness of a tree trunk. Knife-Between-Bones's eyes fluttered open and he drew a ragged breath. Every eye was fixed upon him, unable to shake free of the blasphemous spectacle. The Fenrir held to their line, reluctant to either advance upon or retreat from this monstrosity.

Slowly, the Spiral sat up, prodding and rubbing at his new 'legs' as if they were asleep. Then, putting one arm to the ground to brace himself, he rose unsteadily to his knees.

Not a half pace away, a similar transformation was taking place in what had been the lower half of his body—the severed half, wormlike, regrowing its missing counterpart.

The newly formed face and head of this twin was, as yet, a

featureless white glob, but it turned from side to side as if trying to take in its new surroundings.

It was too much to be borne. With a cry, four of the Fenrir broke ranks and leapt forward to put an end to this abomination. The Warder's invectives fell upon deaf ears. The warriors struck and struck and struck again, as if with mere claw and fang they would carve the monstrous image from their memories.

It was some time before the mass frenzy passed and an uncomfortable silence again descended over the bawn. The bodies of the entire delegation had been shredded in the mad abandon.

The Warder towered over his men, his own rage barely held in check. "Now that bit of foolishness is going to make for a very unpleasant evening. Nobody here—none of you—is going to stir from this spot until every last piece of these three...four... things is accounted for. Once you're absolutely sure that you've got it all, you go over the whole place again because you'll miss something. And one oversight is going to turn into a big problem before morning.

"I want all the remains burned—even the bones—down to a fine ash. After that's done, you come and tell me. I'll be at the House of the Spearsreach. And I want a two-man patrol on this spot all night. You relieve them every hour; I want fresh eyes here until sunup. You know what you're looking for. Don't just stand around, get to work!"

Reluctantly, the patrols set to their grisly task.

The Warder stooped to retrieve the fallen standard where those who had extricated Fimbulwinter from its point had abandoned it. The white banner was stiff with caked blood and ice. Hefting it in one hand, the Warder shook his head and stalked off across the bawn. Almost as an afterthought, he called over his shoulder, "Jorn, you're with me."

Jorn could feel the hostile glares of his fellows boring into his back and knew there would be a reckoning for his having escaped this unpleasant chore so easily. He hurried after the retreating form of the Warder.

Chapter 14

"You tell them what you told me." The Warder, still clutching the bloody standard, shoved Jorn forward. Their sudden appearance had caused quite a commotion in the House of the Spearsreach.

Jorn recovered as gracefully as possible, dropping to one knee before Karin. "A party arrived at the perimeter shortly before sunset, Jarlsdottir," Jorn began uncertainly. "Under a flag of truce. They claimed to be a delegation from Lord Arkady."

At that name a murmuring swept through the hall. Karin's voice cut through the clamor. "A flag of truce? We are not at war with the House of the Crescent Moon. Here is Arkady's own kinsman, Victor Svorenko, seated at table with us." Then the Jarlsdottir's look became suspicious. "Where is this delegation, Jorn Gnaws-Steel, and why have you not brought them before us?"

Jorn shifted uneasily under her scrutiny. "The three were not of House Crescent Moon, Jarlsdottir. They were Black Spiral Dancers."

The hall erupted with cries and accusations.

"Wyrm-taint! A black stain upon all his House."

"What further proof is needed?"

"Did he not command the Knockerwyrm? His own kinsman has admitted as much."

"Even the Spirals run his errands for him!"

Several of the Fenrir warband rose and made a beeline for the doorway. They were only prevented in dashing out across the bawn by the Warder's hulking presence in the opening. The slow, solemn shake of his head told all: The intruders had been dealt with.

Karin struck the butt of her great silver hammer thrice upon the floor to restore some semblance of order. Still there were isolated outbursts.

"What is called for here is clear thinking," Karin said. "Did this delegation offer any proof that they came from Arkady? There is often a chasm between what a Spiral says and what is, in fact, truth."

Jorn considered a moment. "No," he admitted. "Although the spokesman did claim to be a kinsman of Lord Arkady. He said his name was Knife-Between-Bones."

Victor Svorenko was on his feet, his hands slamming down on the table hard enough to rattle the crockery. "I will not have my House slandered in my presence! I came here in good faith, to speak the truth as I have witnessed it. Those of you who last night heard me tell of the fall of Arne Wyrmsbane know that I am not one to shirk the truth—even if it would seem damning to one of my kinsmen. House Crescent Moon is the truest of all the Silver Fang noble lines. This point is uncontested and excru- ciatingly documented. To assert that Lord Arkady is kinsman to such... It is unthinkable. Retract your claim, or defend it with the strength of your arm!"

Jorn bowed slightly in the direction of the incensed Silver Fang. "You mistake me, cousin. I was only reporting the words of the Spiral as I was ordered. I do not myself press this accusa- tion. And it may please you to learn that the Warder has already avenged you this insult."

The bared neck seemed to mollify Victor more than the care- fully chosen words. "I accept your retraction. But have a care to tell us only the exact words of this Knife-Between-Bones, that we can avoid such confusions."

"I will give them to you as nearly as I can remember them," Jorn replied, and proceeded to give a fairly accurate render- ing of the peculiar conversation. When he got to the part about Arkady being "detained," the clamor rose up again, drowning him out.

"This is a foul business," Victor called out. "Arkady has obviously fallen into the clutches of the Spirals. Why else would he not be here by now?"

"Because he is afraid to face us!"

"Who says such?" Victor challenged, reddening. "We must mount a party to track these Wyrm-spawn back to their lair. If Arkady has been taken captive—"

Karin again brought her silver hammer down. "I am sure the Warder already has our best trackers out on the trail," she said. As she scanned the room, however, she saw that Thijs and the others were still present. The Warder had not been at all himself these last weeks, she reflected. The shadow of death rode him mercilessly, goading him on with the lash of vengeance.

Before anyone else could remark on this oversight, she pressed on. "If Arkady fails to present himself, however, we will be forced to pronounce judgment in his absence. We have heard the testimony of Victor Svorenko—Arkady's own kinsman—telling how Arkady commanded the Knockerwyrm and it obeyed him as its master. We have heard the tale of the Silver Crown and how Arkady conspired with the servitors of the Wyrm to capture the throne of Joseph Morningkill for himself. We know that he was forced to flee the States under suspicious circumstances and that this dark cloud followed him all the way home to Russia. And thus far, no one voice—from any of the twelve tribes—has come forward to speak in his defense."

There was a long silence in the hall. It was broken only by the scraping of a chair at the far end of the hall. The young man in a rumpled suit of American cut stood to face the assembly. His long brown hair was drawn back in a ponytail and a flicker of gold at his throat revealed an intricate wolf-headed torc that put one in mind of ancient Irish barrows. When he spoke, however, his voice had an unmistakable Appalachian drawl to it.

"Not one of you, eh? Not a one. Well, it's not hard to tell which way the wind blows through this room. I came a long way hoping to find some answers, but I see nobody here's even asking the questions. Still, I can't very well sit by and see a man condemned without a word spoken to his credit. My given name's Stewart; they call me Stalks-the-Truth.

"Now I don't personally even know this Arkady, but I do know the stories. I know what's in them and I know what's not. And when I hear about Arkady quelling the Knockerwyrm with only his voice, I am put in mind of an old saying, "A house divided against itself cannot stand." You don't cast out devils by the power of the devil and you don't subdue the minions of the Wyrm by the power of the Wyrm. That's in a book somewhere, or near enough. And if I remember the story right, Arkady was not banished after the affair of the Silver Crown. In fact, if he were already under formal censure for his part in that tale, there would be no need for us to sit around passing judgment on him now. No, if Albrecht had it in mind to judge Arkady, he would have done so. There, on the spot. All in all, a few stories is pretty thin evidence on which to convict a man without even giving him his say."

"Our stories are our past, Stewart Stalks-the-Truth," Karin said. "As a law-speaker, I put my trust in the songs and stories of our people. As Arkady has not presented himself, he will be judged by what is said and sung of him—not only by us, but by all who come after. His reputation and his renown must be his defense. It does you credit that you are willing to speak up for him, a stranger to you. I can only wish that there were more voices raised in his praise and fewer in his condemnation."

There were mutters of agreement from around the room. Karin cleared her throat and pitched her voice to carry the length of the hall. "I speak for the Fenrir. It is the judgment of the tribe that Lord Arkady of the House of the Crescent Moon has willingly consorted with the Wyrm and is further complicit in the death of our shield-brother Arne Wyrmsbane. He is from this night declared outcast. No longer shall our halls be open to him, nor shall any of our kinsmen give him aid or succor. His blood is declared already fallen; there shall be no question of *wergild* or any other repercussion against one who is found to have harmed, maimed, or even killed him. We mourn our cousin, fallen in private battle with the Wyrm. Sergiy Dawntreader, how say the Children of Gaia?"

The Dawntreader was seated to Karin's left. One seat separated them, kept empty in honor of Arne Wyrmsbane. To those who watched, it was a visible reminder of the rift that had opened between the two septs.

Only two of his warriors accompanied the Dawntreader

to the moot, each standing surety for five who were pledged. Sergiy remained seated, his head lowered. "I speak for the Sept of the Dawn. My people turn their faces from Lord Arkady of House Crescent Moon. May the grass grow over him and Gaia forgive what we, her chosen, cannot."

Karin nodded solemnly. "Kelonoke Wildhair, how say the Furies?"

"I speak for the Sept of Bygone Visions. Let the mark of Lord Arkady of House Crescent Moon be struck from the record of our people. Let his name be blotted out from the pedigrees and noble lineages of which he was so proud. Let the maenads rend all memory of him from his kin. It is a small mercy."

"Swift-as-the-River," Karin intoned. "How say the Talons?"

The grizzled old wolf that pressed forward through the throng made no answer. He advanced only as far as the hall's central pillar and then, all eyes upon him, lifted one leg and urinated upon the post. Swift-as-the-River turned his back with disdainful flick of the tail and stalked from the hall and out into the night.

Karin's voice broke the eloquent silence. "The Margrave, Yuri Konietzko. How say the Shadow Lords?"

"I speak for my people," the Margrave said, rising to his feet. "It is not our custom to rejoice over fallen rivals, nor to speak ill of the dead. We who are left to hold the front line against the encroachments of the Wyrm will fight on. But we will feel his absence."

"It is done then," Karin said. "Let the word go out among the people." The strength seemed to drain out of her. She leaned heavily upon her silver hammer and hoped that it was not too obvious. To cover her discomfort, she turned and spoke to the Margrave. "I have been giving thought to what you told us yesterday, and your pledge of a return of two score Garou lives on an investment of only ten defenders. It is my intention that you should have the opportunity to make good on that promise. Accordingly, we commit the ten Gaian warriors to your care, to help—as you say—fill the holes left by our fallen comrades. Moreover, I will send a matching force from the collected Fenrir warband, if you think you might be able to find a worthy task for, not ten, but twenty peerless warriors."

"I thank you, Karin Jarlsdottir," the Margrave replied. "I think I might. We have already heard from Kelonoke Wildhair about a new threat making itself felt in the Balkans. There can be little doubt that the Wyrm is making inroads in this region and sorely pressing us on several fronts. If you are of a like mind, we can send the bulk of this contingent to reinforce our position in the Balkans while sending a handpicked few to investigate the source of the renewed Wyrm activity there."

"An excellent plan. How does this sound to you, Kelonoke Wildhair? Does the Margrave's proposal address your concerns?"

"It does, Jarlsdottir. I am content to place this matter in his hands."

Seated at the Fury's right hand, Mari shot Kelonoke a sharp glance. She could hear the rehearsed tones in the familiar voice. *Is this what you meant by your devil's bargain?* she wondered. *Not a pact with the enemy, but with someone who might prove even more dangerous.*

"And if the Dawntreader has no objections?" Karin said.

"The gift is given freely, without conditions or strings attached. The ten go where the Jarlsdottir commands. If they are allowed to fight by the Fenrir's side, so much the better."

"Then it is settled," Karin said. "All that remains is to pick the handful that will go into peril."

"I will go." The commanding voice came from the rear of the hall. The assembly turned as one to stare at the Warder.

"It is out of the question," Karin replied. "Your duties—"

"I resign my duties effective at the close of this moot."

"I see," Karin replied carefully. An uneasy silence fell. She could see the Warder's doom champing at his heels, driving him relentlessly before it. "The rest of your pack will accompany you, then. Jorn Gnaws-Steel, Fangs-First, Mars-Rising, Fimbulwinter, Aeric Bleeds-Only-Ice..." She ticked off the names on the fingers of one hand. "You leave our perimeter sorely undermanned."

"It won't kill the hunters to pull a shift or two. At least until Mountainsides can train up some capable replacements. Things may be a bit strained all around for a while. You've pledged ten warriors."

"She's pledged her share of ten," Jotun Threeships laughed. "You can't expect us to let you lot garner the alpha's share of the glory. Besides, we've been doing this longer than you have. We're far better at it."

"That remains to be seen," came a rejoinder from the crowd.

Some ways down the table, Mari rose to her feet. "I'm going with you." Her tone preempted any argument. Seeing the skeptical look on the Warder's face, however, she added, "I made a promise of my own. If your people were dying down there, you would be there."

The invocation of the dead must have gotten through to the Warder. Outwardly, he only shrugged dismissively, as if he really hadn't the time to argue further. "You can follow as long as you make yourself useful. But only that long." Then he turned and began giving detailed orders to Jorn. There was much to do and few able hands left to do it.

"One thing is bothering me," said the Margrave.

"What is that?" Karin said.

"Only this: That often the root of a problem is not to be found in the physical world at all, but rather in the spiritual. It is often said that if a tree is blighted in the Umbral realm, its physical manifestation cannot help but wither and die. So it is with many problems: To heal a wound in this world, it is often necessary to root out the canker in the next."

"What is it that you suggest?" Karin asked.

"I propose a further refinement to your excellent plan. In addition to the pack that will venture into the heart of the Balkans to physically uncover the newly awakened evil that Kelonoke Wildhair warned us of, we also send a second pack to investigate the problem from an Umbral vantage point. A certain avenue of attack suggests itself to me, centering around a lost pathstone from one of the caerns along the Tisza River basin that has—despite valiant resistance—been recently overrun. But we will speak more of these details later in a more private venue."

"So we shall," Karin replied. "I find your suggestion a most auspicious one. Two packs: body and soul, the physical and the spiritual."

"A tripod with but two legs topples," came an ominous voice from near the fire. "And woe to him who shelters beneath such an ill-fated scheme." Necks craned to try to pick out the speaker. A middle-aged man, with a face as crisscrossed with lines as an old fishing net, sat staring into the flames. His skin was tanned and leathery, his face sported a three-day growth of beard. He looked like a man who had lived most of his life on an exposed mountainside.

"The Fates are three," he continued, speaking into the flames, oblivious to the attention turned upon him. "And the Furies, three. Luna herself has three faces: Virgin, Mother and Crone. And the old Wyrm has three segments: Beast-of-War, Eater-of-Souls and Defiler Wyrm. All of creation is a Triat: Weaver, Wyrm and Wyld. And Gaia's children, they have three aspects as well. But only two can they remember. They see her, yes. They certainly feel her. Now why, I wonder, can they not remember?"

"Who speaks thus, reproving the Garou for forgetfulness? Stand forward," Jotun Threeships challenged.

The man at the fireside cocked his head as if only hearing them from a great distance. Then he rose slowly to his feet and turned to begin making his way toward the head table. His progress was torturous, his limp pronounced, and he nearly stumbled each time his right foot hit the floor. Threeships grew both impatient at the slow progress and embarrassed at having called out a cripple. "Thor's sake, someone give the man a hand!" One of his warriors hurried forward and put an arm around the man's shoulder.

The lame man smiled sheepishly and took one hesitant step forward. Pleased with the results, he took another and then another, until the pair were boldly and rapidly striding across the hall. All trace of the earlier limp had vanished. The two looked like a pair of old drinking buddies, arm-in-arm, hurrying on toward the next alehouse.

"Ah, that's all it needed was another leg," the stranger said, slapping his companion on the back. "A man can barely stand on two legs, but give him a third and he'll go places."

They had arrived at the High Table and the enigmatic man bowed low before his hosts. "I am called Antonine Teardrop. I thank you for your hospitality. In return, you are welcome to my Riddle of Threes. If you heed it, you might yet save your people a great calamity."

"You say there is something that we have forgotten," Karin said. "Some oversight in the Margrave's plan?"

"No, *you* said that," Antonine correctly gently. "But you say rightly."

"Or do you mean," the Margrave said, "that there is something that we have forgotten as a people? Some knowing that is lost to us?"

"And that also is spoken rightly. And the longer you do not act, the more knowing slips from you. This much I have seen. Perhaps more. It is so hard to recall."

"You must speak plainly," called Jotun Threeships in exasperation. "I can't make heads nor tails of your words. If you mean to warn us, you will have to do a better job of it."

"Very well, I will strike a bargain with you. I will speak my warning more plainly if, in return, you will grant me a boon."

"What boon is it that you ask, Antonine Teardrop?" Karin asked shrewdly.

"Only this: that when you discover what must be done, you will allow me to chose who will do it."

Karin glanced at the Margrave and he shrugged, feigning disinterest. "Done," she said.

Antonine bowed. "Excellent. The meaning of the Riddle of Three is this—that like our patron, Luna, the Garou have a triune nature. We are body and spirit, yes. But we are something more. We are a repository of memory, creatures of the Litany and the Record. We are story and song, history and tradition. Any quest, such as the one you have outlined, that does not take this third aspect into account, is doomed not only to fail, but ultimately to be forgotten."

"A third pack," Karin said, comprehension dawning. "Body, Spirit and Mind. But what will this third pack do?"

"It must search for the root of the problem among the

detritus of the Garou's past," Antonine replied. "Sometimes only by going backward can you go forward."

More riddles. Karin laughed and shook her head. "Very well, Antonine Teardrop. We will accept your good counsel and form a third pack. But we must make good on our promise of a boon. Who would you have undertake this enigmatic mission?"

"That is easy enough," Antonine replied. "The fosterling, the one that is called Cries Havoc."

"No, he will not." The Warder's hard voice broke over the assembly. His long strides rapidly closed the distance to the High Table. "The fosterling's life is not his own. It is mine. I have demanded the bloodprice for the life of my son."

"And they have paid the bloodprice. In the coin of ten Gaian warriors," Antonine suggested calmly.

"They claimed that that was a gift to honor the dead, not an atonement," the Warder said. "The bloodprice remains due. I appeal to the Jarlsdottir."

Karin sighed and rubbed her eyes. "Have the fosterling brought here. He should hear this, he deserves that much." Then she turned her attention back to Antonine. "It is as the Warder says, Antonine Teardrop. The bloodprice is not yet paid. Furthermore, although you may select Cries Havoc to go on this mission, you must also realize that the fosterling may not be alive to undertake it."

Antonine scratched at his beard. "Living or dead, it makes little difference. I select him. The Silver Pack will not coalesce around any other."

A gust of cold air blew through the hall as the door was thrown back. Two figures entered, leaning heavily on one another. The curving ram's horns immediately identified the first as Cries Havoc. The second was his charge, the wounded Fenrir warrior, Aeric Bleeds-Only-Ice.

"They go on three legs!" came a sharp whisper from the assembly. "Just as the seer said."

Slowly, the two made their way to the High Table. Cries Havoc bowed his head first to the Jarlsdottir, and then to the Dawntreader. But it was the Warder he addressed.

"I give your warrior back to you, Warder. It is the least I

could do in return for the kindness you have showed me. I am glad there was time enough before the end. I am ready to die now, for the peace between our peoples."

"For Luna's sake, let us finish this!" the Warder growled wearily. In truth, he no longer had much of an appetite for this killing. But he would go through with it to see justice done. He would do so for his son's honor and perhaps so that he himself might find, in appeasing the restless dead, some small measure of relief from the oppressive weight that bore down upon him.

"Cries Havoc," Karin pronounced. "You know your life stood as guarantee against that of Arne Wyrmsbane and that he was killed while under the protection of your people. You understood this arrangement from the outset and entered into it willingly. You have declared yourself ready to die for the peace between our peoples, and that is well spoken. Now I must ask you, will you abide by my sentence, no matter how onerous?"

"I will, Jarlsdottir. I am yours to command. It has been thus since the day I first came here and Sergiy Dawntreader committed my life into your hands."

"Kneel," she commanded.

Cries Havoc went to his knees before her, baring the back of his neck.

Karin hefted her silver law-speaker's hammer. With both hands, she swung it up to shoulder height. In her human form, it was no easy feat even to lift the massive hammer, much less swing it overhead.

"Cries Havoc, I commend your spirit to Great Fenris-Wolf. May he shelter you in his jaws and raise you up again—by the scruff of your neck—on the last day."

At these words, a mournful howl went up among the Fenrir warband. It filled the House of the Spearsreach. The Jarlsdottir's hammer arced and flashed silver, hovering for a moment at the very crux of its swing. Then it came down upon the back of the fosterling's head. He crumpled to the floor.

Karin let the head of the hammer sink to the ground beside him. It dangled forgotten from the end of one arm.

Sergiy Dawntreader, like most of the assembly, was already on his feet. Now he stooped over the body. Karin laid a hand on his shoulder.

"It is enough, Dawntreader. The cub is dead to you now. Your people can be proud; he died well and for a cause he believed in." There were tears in the corners of his eyes as he turned away.

"Aeric Bleeds-Only-Ice," she called.

Startled, the injured warrior came haltingly forward. "This little one nursed you back to health. You will stand watch over him." He nodded solemnly and knelt over the body.

"Warder, you have your bloodprice. Go home now, get some rest. It is done."

"But Jarlsdottir, I must stay. How will he know..."

"He will know. Go."

With a bow, the Warder turned and left the hall.

All that remained now was to stand vigil over the body. There was not a sound from the assembly. No one stirred from his place.

It was an hour after moonset that the solemn silence was broken. A long, low moan.

"Jarlsdottir!" Aeric's excited whisper followed hot on its heels. A press of bodies crowded closer.

Cries Havoc moaned again and put one hand to his head. He found only Aeric's hand, holding the bandage firmly in place. He pawed at it uncomprehendingly.

"You didn't hit him hard enough," Threeships laughed. "You'll have to give him another one. Here, let me have a go at him."

Cries Havoc's head came up in alarm. He instantly regretted the gesture. Aeric caught him before his head could hit the floor again.

"Jotun!" Karin scolded and then, in a softer voice. "It's all right, Cries Havoc. You are safe now. Grandfather Wolf has raised you up for us. The bloodprice is paid. You are dead to your old tribe now. Do you understand? You are one of us. One of the Fenrir."

At these words a jubilant howl went up from the assembly.

Threeships thunked his axe into the nearest cask and strong drink flowed freely. There was a great clashing of cups and armaments. The room erupted in sound and motion.

Runners streaked from the doorway to bring the glad news to the rest of the sept. The cry was taken up by each of the patrols along the perimeter, passed along the lines like a summons to battle. It swelled in volume and intensity, echoed back from every point of the compass. Stragglers on the Aeld Baile, looking up, bared their throats to Luna, adding their voices to the cry of elation. The song caught like tinder and raced through even the heartwood where their wildest brethren ran and not even a Garou dared be caught out wearing a human skin this night.

In this way, the Fenrir sang the rebirth of their shield-brother.

Curious about other Crossroad Press books?
Stop by our site:
https://www.crossroadpress.com
We offer quality writing
in digital, audio, and print formats.